PHANTOM ISLE

A WATERWAY CHRONICLE ADVENTURE

BOOK 2

BY MATTHEW GORE

Phantom Isle, A Waterway Chronicle Adventure
Book 2

Copyright © 2024 Matthew Gore

Paperback ISBN: 979-8-9911138-0-9

Cover Design: Thom Hoyman

Dedication

This book is dedicated to:

My parents, David and Aundrea Gore.

I grew up in a middle class family. Dad worked hard. Sometimes too hard, but he wanted good things for our family. Mom made a home for us, and my sister and I always knew one thing without doubt: we were deeply loved. Now, after navigating the world for fifty-nine years, experiencing the ups and downs, I'm thankful every day for what a charmed life they made possible.

"You can do anything you put your mind to, son."

Parents, those are the most powerful words in the world.

Now married sixty years, and far from perfect, my folks are still a steadfast example of how to do family.

I love you both, very much.

Chapter 1

I FORCED THE COMPACTED AIR from my lungs and opened my eyes to the endless cobalt-blue sky broken only by a few wispy white clouds. Flat on my back, I lay wondering what I'd missed—again.

Consistent with his style, Morgan had no mercy, and this was the second time in three minutes he'd flipped me to the mat on the foredeck.

"Michael, you're telegraphing your move with your feet," Morgan said.

"I'm not sure how to telegraph with my feet, but I'll take your word for it."

Morgan, a former DEV Group operator, was putting part of the crew through yet another training session he insisted we conduct on a regular basis. This type of training for me began years ago as I started my career as a conflict journalist and was traveling to some of the most dangerous environments around the world. With the assignments I began taking from the networks, Morgan knew I would eventually encounter serious trouble, and he wanted his twin brother to be prepared for the things that most journalists were not.

I left that nightmare world almost a decade ago, but with Morgan's military background and training, he was still adamant the entire crew stay in shape. The crew that was suspect of the often intense training in the beginning now embraced the sessions, and I could see the added confidence it had built in everyone.

We couldn't have picked more ideal conditions to be on deck. A spectacular sunrise had given way to a beautiful mild afternoon in early December with a slight westerly breeze, flat seas, and seventy-four degree temps. The kind of day that made me feel invincible. It was ironic that I felt so confident lying on my back on the deck, but I did, because I *would* get up and we *would* go again.

Morgan and I were co-owners of Water Horse Expeditions, and you wouldn't think the crew of a marine research vessel specializing in high-end videography and exploration would need to be skilled in close combat defense, but the experience on our last assignment had made me even more grateful that we trained whenever possible.

"Come on, Michael. You'll get him this time," Jas, our onboard tech and network specialist, said, clapping her hands and urging me on like a coach motivating a player lying in the mud to get back in the game. I looked up and half-grinned at her and Beau Benson, our newest crew member, standing over me at the edge of the mat.

The one-hundred-forty-foot, navy-blue hull of our home and office, *Water Horse*, made an easy ten knots through the clear turquoise water. Our heading was north-northwest, one hundred nautical miles off the coast of Nicaragua, bound for Cancun, a little over thirty hours away at our current speed. We were en route to begin a new assignment. This project was out of the norm from our previous expedition experience. But the request came from a legitimate government entity and the contract price was attractive. I had made a pact with myself to never take an assignment based on the pay. And although the compensation offered here was fantastic, the most important thing to me, this go around, was this assignment would keep the boat and crew working and carry us all comfortably through the holidays and into the New Year. And on top of that . . . it was in warm water! So here we were, heading to Cancun.

I rolled to my feet quickly and raised my sparring gloves, ready for another shot to best the teacher.

"Remember to keep eye contact. Part of the technique on a leg sweep is the aggressiveness of the upper body contact as you sweep the leg," Morgan said.

I advanced, striking with several left-right jab combos as Morgan defended. Morgan countered with a blindingly quick combo himself, but my experience was growing and I bobbed and deflected his punches with my raised forearms. As Morgan stepped back to regroup, I shot toward him, slamming my right shoulder into his upper body, positioning my right arm high across his chest. As I brought my right foot around behind Morgan's right leg to sweep it, his leg wasn't there. The next sensation was a quick blur of blue mat, followed by my repeated view of tropical blue sky.

"Better!" Morgan said.

"Better?" I chuckled, lying on the deck. "How was that better?"

"You almost got me, and your action was much smoother and more explosive," Morgan said.

Jas extended her hand to help me up. "I thought you had him that time," she said, smiling as she pulled me to my feet. "You *are* getting much faster."

"Thanks, but not fast enough—yet," I said.

"Okay, Jas you and Beau, on the mat," Morgan said.

Beau, a former marine, was injured on our last assignment. He'd healed well and trained constantly on the trip down from Alaska. By all indications, he was back to full strength and then some. Beau was six feet tall, and I guessed about a hundred eighty-five pounds of hard, lean muscle. Jas was a sinewy five foot four and no more than one-thirty. She was a former world champion free diver, in amazing shape, and an absolute force of nature.

The two faced one another on the mat and began slowly circling, watching the other's movements while each planned their first strike. The by far out-sized Jas took the initiative and landed a series of jabs that Beau defended well, but the surprise on his face at Jas's speed and power was undeniable. Beau countered with a series of powerful punches that ended with a strong front kick. Jas brushed and blocked the blows, keeping herself out of the range of any contact. The ballet for position continued as the two were moving around each other on the mat, and that's when I saw it. Jas grinned one split second before she lunged at Beau like a striking snake. She impacted his midsection with her shoulder. Her forearm shot up, braced high on his chest as her right foot expertly fired around Beau's right foot. Then she executed the leg sweep I'd been unsuccessfully trying moments before on Morgan. Jas's result was much different, Beau's six-foot, bulky mass, hit the mat like a sack of potatoes. He lay on his back stunned, and as Jas extended her hand to him, he chuckled. I gave Morgan a wide-eyed look, and he returned the look with a smile and a wink.

"Fish on! Fish on!" Rudy yelled from the stern.

Rudy was our ship's engineer and resident old salt. In a rarely witnessed display of anything resembling downtime, he was fishing. I turned and yelled up to Jerry Styles in the pilothouse at the helm, "Fish On!" Jerry gave me a thumbs up and dropped us back to idle speed.

We all dropped our sparring gloves onto the mat and rushed down the side deck toward the stern to find Rudy locked in mortal combat with something big and unhappy. The reel's drag screamed as the fish stripped the line running for the bottom.

"Whatcha got there, Rudy?" I asked.

"I'm not sure, Cap, but it feels big—and pissed!" Rudy strained to hang on to the large trolling rod that was bent into a tight J.

Rudy was wearing a short-sleeved T-shirt, and I over-heard Beau whisper to Jas: "Dang! Look at the guns on Rudy. He's like almost fifty, right?"

Smiling, Jas just kept watching the tug-of-war. "Rudy is the real deal. You think I put you on the mat fast? If you ever lock horns with that gray-haired honey badger, you'll under-stand real trouble."

Beau gave Rudy's biceps another long look as the silver-haired engineer powerfully pumped the heavy rod, reeling to gain back some line on the big fish. "Roger *that*," Beau said.

The drag on a second reel standing in a rod holder on the stern rail screamed to life. It was a double hook up. "Jas, grab that rod," Rudy grunted, as he pulled against his own catch. Jas sprang to the stern and snatched the rod from the holder.

"Whoo hoo!" she yelled, as her tanned, muscled arms strained against the pull of another big game fish on the line. "I can taste the fillets already!" The rod bent over double when the fish made a hard run.

"Watch your drag, Jas. He's running," Morgan called.

Jas made a slight adjustment to the drag as it screamed and she took her hand off the reel to grip the bent rod with both hands.

Our marine must have felt left out of the action, and he shouted, "Hey Jas, you need any—"

I put my arm on Beau's shoulder. "You don't want to go there, buddy."

"Get 'em, Jas. You're doing great!" he said.

I nodded with approval.

The battle went on for another fifteen minutes while we all cheered and encouraged our anglers as they pulled and reeled, slowly turning the tide of the man vs. beast contest in their favor. Rudy's fish came up first.

"Somebody wanna grab a gaff? I think he's about done," Rudy said.

"I got it," I said, while pulling the gaff off its brackets mounted on the main cabin bulkhead, and trotted toward the boarding platform on the port stern. As Rudy pulled the fish closer to the boat, the sun reflected off the fish's beautiful turquoise and yellow head and back, that glided just beneath the surface of the clear water. The large bull Mahi looked to be at least fifty pounds.

"Almost there, Rudy, just another few feet," I said.

"Yep, here he comes," Rudy grunted.

Rudy pulled the line and the fish up against the platform and I extended the gaff and hooked the big lunker, pulling him up onto the platform. The Mahi was heavy. I called out to Beau. "Hey, can I hand this big boy up to you?"

Beau reached over the stern rail as I extended the long end of the gaff toward him.

"I got him!" Beau said, as he heaved the big fish up and over the rail with a grunt.

Cheers went up as Beau laid the big fish on the deck. Beau handed the gaff back to me as Jas's fish was close behind. I waited for her to maneuver it close enough to the platform for me to reach it with the gaff. It was another beauty. Not quite as big as Rudy's, but easily forty pounds and beautifully colored. "Don't you miss my fish, Cap."

"You just keep bringing him this way, hot shot, don't worry about me."

A few more feet and Jas had pulled him close enough for me to reach. I gaffed him and Beau pulled him up over the rail and on deck and laid the big Mahi next to the first. I came up from the platform and slapped Rudy on the back as he caught his breath. "Nice job! I like mine with extra butter and a little Cajun spice, by the way."

"Oh, we're gonna eat like kings tonight, for sure," Rudy said, still breathing hard.

"You too, Jas, nice work," I said.

Jas was barely out of breath and her smile was like a five-year-old kid at Christmas. "I used to fish all the time with my dad off the panhandle of Florida. I didn't realize just how much I missed it."

"Well, dinner tonight is compliments of you and Rudy, so thank you," I said.

"I have a tropical bean salad that'll go great with grilled fillets," Ellie said. Our younger sister was on board in some rare time off as an investigative journalist for the *New York Times*. She had met me in Panama as *Water Horse* cleared the eastern end of the Panama canal and she'd be tagging along until we docked in Cancun.

"You're on, Ellie," Rudy said. "You know where everything is in the galley. Have at it. I'll get these beasts cleaned, cut into fillets, and on the grill."

Today would go into the hall of fame of good days. The sun, the breeze, and beautiful water blended with the people I cared about. Add fresh caught Mahi while sitting around a rowdy dinner table, and I wanted to savor every second of it. Further down in my gut, I also had to admit it was a somewhat beautiful distraction. Something about our new assignment had been nagging at me from the dark, quiet little corners of my mind, and I just couldn't get a firm grip on it.

Chapter 2

IT SEEMED HARD TO BELIEVE that only a few weeks earlier I was peering through a small window as I descended into the smog of Mexico City. Morgan never liked to be involved with the contract end of the operation. So after several packed flights and delayed connections, AeroMexico finally delivered me into the swirling chaos that nine million souls called home. The cab ride from the airport was scarier than most things I experienced in war zones overseas, and it ended with a skidding stop in front of my hotel. Relieved to be alive, I checked into my room, then checked my phone to find a nearby men's shop, because I needed to pick up some nicer clothes. I had never met with government officials interested in our services before, and I didn't think my normal boat-wear would leave the best first impression.

A navy sport coat, tan slacks, dress shirt, and new shoes set me back two hundred bucks, but this had the potential to be a profitable assignment and now I'd actually have some client-worthy clothes. At nine the next morning, I sat in a very nice government office in the heart of Mexico City in a nice shirt. I silently laughed to myself, because for the life of me, I couldn't remember the last time I actually wore a dress shirt. My invitation had come by way of the Mexican Secretary of the Ministry of Energy, Secretaría de Energía, a Ms. Mariana Vega. When my host entered the room, her presence made an immediate impression. Ms. Vega was tall, slim, impeccably dressed—and beautiful. She wore her long black hair in a tight braid that descended below the center of her back, and her English was much better than mine.

"Mr. Gannon, thank you so much for traveling to Mexico. You've come highly recommended in the marine exploration circles," she said, extending her hand to deliver a very firm handshake.

"Thank you, Ms. Vega. Please call me Michael."

"Very well, Michael."

We both took our seats as an assistant entered the room with coffee for Ms. Vega, and she asked, "Can we get you some coffee this morning, señor Gannon?"

"No, thank you. I got an early start today."

"Very well. If you change your mind, let us know," the young assistant said as she exited, closing the door.

"Ms. Vega, your deputy said that this was regarding boundary-water explorations off your Yucatán coast. Is that correct?"

"It is indeed, but as with most border issues, there's always a tricky wrinkle. And this one starts several hundred years ago. Since around the eighteenth century, Spanish explorers charted the island of Bermeja approximately two hundred kilometers off the coast of Yucatán on the edge of the Campeche Bank. The 1921 edition of the Geographic Atlas of the Mexican Republic recorded its position yet again. But as the US and Mexico began renegotiating maritime boundaries as it related to oil exploration rights in the Gulf of Mexico, the island of Bermeja . . . was gone."

"I'm sorry, Ms. Vega, did you say, gone?"

"I did, Mr. Gannon—Michael. After two extensive surveys, the uninhabited island of Bermeja was nowhere to be found."

"How big was Bermeja?" I asked.

"Only two hundred hectares, and of course, uninhabited. Many of our scientists and I believe the island was misidentified in the early surveys or because of its size, that natural erosion and storms in the Gulf simply washed it away. However, many individuals in our government believe that something more suspect is involved in the island's disappearance."

"Because it would change your territorial borders, giving you decreased reach into the Gulf for oil exploration," I said.

"Precisely."

"Ms. Vega, taking into account that you've already conducted two surveys, a couple of questions immediately come to mind. One, what do you think my team and I can do to help the Mexican government? And two, why hire an American company to conduct this research?"

"I chose your company precisely because you are not from Mexico or affiliated with the Mexican government. More importantly, you have no previous association with the petroleum industry. This situation is politically charged, and I believe that even though you are an American, your extensive work internationally allows you to offer an unbiased perspective."

"Fair enough," I said. "But Secretary Vega, Bermeja has still been missing for some time now. Why look now?"

Ms. Vega took a sip from her coffee and precisely placed it back on the saucer on her desk. "Well, Michael, now it seems that another small island off the Yucatán has disappeared."

Wide-eyed, I said, "That is interesting."

"Again, these are very small islands, only a foot above

sea level, so natural causes seem to be the most likely answer."

"But people in your government suspect something more?"

"Any time governments negotiate or change drilling exploration agreements, a staggering amount of oil revenue is at stake. So it's not surprising that some of my fellow government officials are quite distressed."

"If the islands didn't simply erode or get washed away by storms, what do some of your colleagues think happened to the islands?"

"The theories range from sabotage by big oil in the US to covert plots by your CIA."

"Whoa, that seems like a stretch."

"I agree, but with a second island now in question, there is too much oil revenue at stake to not investigate this thoroughly."

"Does this new missing island have a name?"

"It does. Isla Escondida." She smiled.

"Hidden Island? That seems appropriate." I chuckled.

"Yes, the irony is—uncanny."

"Back to my previous question, Ms. Vega. What can Water Horse Expeditions do to help the Ministry of Energy?"

"We'd like to put one of our lead marine geologist with your team and use his expertise with your added fresh perspective to confirm these islands are indeed disappearing from natural causes or investigate the unlikely chance that there's—something else going on in the Gulf waters off our coast."

I wasn't sure what it was in the way she made the statement, but something in it made the hairs on the back of my neck stand up.

Ms. Vega pressed a button on her desk phone and said, "Elena, will you have Dr. Cruz join us, please?"

"Sí, señora Vega."

The office door opened and a man, close to six feet tall, well-tanned, with a million-dollar smile, entered the office. I rose to meet him and extended my hand. "Dr. Cruz, Michael Gannon, nice to meet you."

Dr. Cruz took my hand and flashed his almost too perfect white teeth. "Michael, it is very nice to meet you. I am familiar with some of your excellent work filming in the Mediterranean during archaeological discoveries there. I've also heard many great things about your vessel, the *Water Horse*. What attracts you to the unglamourous work of digging in the sands of the Gulf of Mexico with me is a mystery, but I very much look forward to working with you."

"My crew and I will work very hard to provide you all the support you need, Dr. Cruz."

"Am I correct you were involved in solving the very sudden disappearance of king crab in the Bering Sea recently?"

His statement fired my alert senses, making my forehead tingle. We were not mentioned in any of Ellie's articles about the king crab incident. The fact that he had that information so soon after our time in Alaska meant he clearly had done research on the Water Horse team. On first blush, I didn't think I liked him.

"It was fortunate we could help that community. It's an important fishery," I said.

With his smile set to a ten, Dr. Cruz said, "Ah, señora Vega, our Mr. Gannon is quite modest. Despite the fact he is an outsider, perhaps together, we can discover what happened to our phantom isles, yes?"

Chapter 3

MUSIC FILLED THE GALLEY of the *Water Horse* and the melodies of Buffett, Marley, and Steely Dan mixed magically with the raucous voices of our crew. We took turns passing mounded platters of fresh fish around a table covered in other side dishes and tropical libations. Ellie fit in well with the crew and it was good to see her having such a great time. Morgan had relieved Jerry Styles, at the helm, so now, our first officer joined the five of us for the seafood feast that Rudy and Ellie had prepared. I'd take a heaping plate to Morgan in the pilothouse as soon as I gorged a little myself. Meals like this were some of my favorite memories of home in coastal South Carolina. Weekends in the late spring when we fished around pilings and bridges on the intercoastal, we could catch our limit of redfish before noon, net some shrimp on the way back to the dock, and be surrounded by friends and family eating the best fresh catch ever, before five.

Ellie sat with her eyes closed, just finishing a bite. "Mmm. Rudy, this is the best fish I think I've ever put in my mouth!"

"Sunshine, fresh caught, and good friends make everything taste a little better, doesn't it?"

"It certainly does tonight," she said, forking in another bite.

"Nice work on this tropical salad. You're welcome in the galley anytime, Ellie."

Ellie beamed. "I wish I could stay longer, but there's New York rent to pay and big stories to break. Michael, you've not said much about this new assignment. Any chance there's a story in this one?"

I spent a few minutes summarizing my meeting with Energy Secretary Vega and Bermeja's disappearance. As usual, Ellie asked the first pointed question, "Did you find it odd that Mexico would hire a group based in America for the project?"

"The secretary said the fact that we were outside the government and didn't have any experience in the petroleum industry would give the project a fresh perspective."

The rest of the group nodded with acceptance. Ellie gave

a slight tilt of her head and a "hmm," so I wasn't sure if she bought the explanation or not. Now, after repeating it out loud, I couldn't deny it made my mental gears spin more than I wanted to admit.

The crew continued listening as I relayed more details of the different outlandish theories and political tensions surrounding the situation. Even though they appeared distracted by chewing and dishing extra helpings, when I got to the part about a second missing island, everyone stopped eating and looked at me.

"Two islands have disappeared?" Beau asked.

"It seems so," I said, taking a slow sip of a very tasty Doc Swinson bourbon.

"What's the name of the second island?" Ellie asked.

"Isla Escondida," I answered.

"Isla Escondida . . . Hidden Island?" Jas asked, eyebrow raised.

"Yeah, ironic, I know. These are tiny islands, most without names at all, but dry territorial land is just that . . . land. And land establishes maritime borders, which determines where Mexico can explore for oil in the Gulf."

Ellie pulled out her phone and began rapidly thumb-typing. "Okay, slow your roll there, sis. It's almost certain that this is nothing more than erosion and Gulf storms washing these small sand spits back into the Gulf," I said.

"You *are* the same brother that just found a Cold War-era submarine vacuuming crab off the bottom of the Bering Sea, right?"

Guilty. But I didn't want Ellie mounting a big hairy investigation yet. I had a small itch in the back of my mind that hadn't grown into a full nag just yet. The sight of Ellie eagerly combing the dark web for information in a blur of thumbs may the itch grow, and it was too early for that. We'd do the job we'd been contracted to do and follow the evidence along the way.

"Who's the guy we're meeting in Cancun?" Beau asked.

"He's a marine geologist, Dr. Mateo Cruz," I answered. "Lots of tan and teeth."

"Sounds interesting." Jas smiled.

I rolled my eyes. "He'll be running the science concerning the geology of the area, collecting bottom soil samples, and so on. We'll document the research with stills and video, supervise dive operations, and put the ROV to work."

"So they want us to help find out what really happened to the islands?" Jerry asked.

"Yes, and see if we think anything other than natural circumstances is involved," I answered.

"Ahh, like what?" Beau asked.

Ellie's thumb-typing stopped abruptly as she smiled up at me, awaiting my answer.

I'd seen that look many times. Including that day that I was supposed to have dropped her at the library after school, but instead, opted to run to the beach with some buddies and dented the fender on Mom's car backing out of a parking space on the hurried trip home. It was a very small ding, so I parked the car without mentioning it. Dad hadn't been in the door twenty seconds when I heard him call from the living room, "Who dented Mom's car?" Ellie, Morgan, Mom, and I sat at the table waiting for Dad to start dinner, and Ellie's smile beamed as Dad entered the dining room.

It was the same look tonight. I charged on confidently. "It seems that there are a few members of the government administration that would like to blame US oil companies or the CIA."

"For making two whole islands disappear?" Jas asked.

I shrugged my shoulders.

Rudy chuckled. "Well, that's a big 'aww shit.'"

The crew broke into laughter and Ellie's thumbs resumed the hummingbird-wing-flitter across her phone's keypad.

I prepared a heaping plate and carefully balanced it as I took the stairs to the pilothouse. Morgan sat in the helm seat, and I set his plate of fresh catch and sides on the nav station.

"The fish is amazing. Sorry you didn't get to sit down with the group. It was a feast for sure."

"Yeah, I know, it sounded like fun down there, but then I would have missed this." Morgan pointed through the forward pilothouse windows toward the setting sun, that was only seconds away from slipping under the horizon. The warm dry air of the last few weeks made for spectacular reds and maroons that reflected off the calm waters of the far western Caribbean to create a painting no human could ever replicate.

"Makes a fella feel blessed," he said. We both basked in the moment, mesmerized by the incredible sight that punctuated the end of a glorious day.

Finally, Morgan asked, "Did you brief the team on where we're headed?"

"I gave them the highlights. Ellie was typing notes like she's already on the job."

"I bet," Morgan said. "Think there's anything here other than Mother Nature doing her thing?"

"Probably not, but there's tens of millions of oil dollars at stake, so that always makes me a little suspicious. Dr. Cruz will come aboard once we reach Cancun, and we'll have him give a more detailed brief to the team."

"Sounds like a plan," Morgan said. "So since you were able to sit down for dinner, think you can relieve me at midnight?"

"Fair enough," I said. "Enjoy your dinner. I'm going to

sit on the bow for a while as the stars come out—it really was a great day."

Out on deck, the last dim glows of the fiery sunset surrendered to the horizon in the west. Sirius, the Dog Star, blinked into view as it began its trek across the night sky. I stood leaning against the rail on the port side, just breathing in the salty breeze and enjoying the evening. Jas walked up, turned, and leaned against the rail next to me. Her arm brushed against mine, and the touch of her warm, freshly tanned skin shot a wave of warmth through my arm and across my chest. My forehead tingled like it'd been in the sun. It felt good— very good in fact. She didn't say a word. We just stood quietly for several long minutes as more and more stars became visible in the eastern sky. It's one of the things I liked about her. She was never uncomfortable with silence.

After several quiet moments, she sighed. "I wish I could make a thousand days in a row just like today."

"Me too, sometimes," I said. "But I guess it's those other days that make one like this seem so great."

"Probably so, but I wouldn't mind doing the research on that theory."

We both laughed a little, then sat silently, watching as more stars revealed themselves in the darkening curtain of the tropical night.

The chemistry . . . or awkwardness for me and Jas had increased in recent weeks. I felt like a bumbling fool during most any moment of sustained eye contact or subtle brushes in hatchways. Jas seemed to find it all very entertaining. My horrible relationship track record of the last ten years may have been the reason for my reluctance to push things any further. I was never home in DC before moving aboard *Water Horse* and when I was home, by the time any relationship showed promise, I was off on another assignment. There was one close call with a pretty blonde researcher from Nat Geo. Things progressed and we seemed very compatible. But the call came and I was assigned overseas for a four-week run. One week into my time in Thailand, and the inevitable "I don't think it'll work" email arrived right on schedule. Then there was the fact that I was the captain, Jas's boss . . . kinda. Jas was one of the most talented tech specialists I had ever met and I had tremendous respect for her professionally and personally. If I screwed that up, I'd lose twice. For now, it'd just have to stay awkward.

I was about to excuse myself to close my eyes in my cabin for a few hours before my watch at midnight when Jas grabbed my arm, catching me off guard.

"Michael, what is that?" she said, pointing to the water off our starboard bow.

In the light of the half-full moon, I could just make out something in the water about a quarter mile away. I rushed toward the steps leading to the pilothouse, taking them two at a time. When I stepped inside, Morgan answered before I spoke.

"Yeah, I see it. It was making the tiniest target on the radar. I was just waiting to get a little closer to see what it was."

Morgan cut the throttles back to idle speed as we came closer to the object, and now we could both see that it was a small boat. As it came within fifty yards of our bow, Morgan flipped a switch on the instrument panel, illuminating a spotlight on the mast, and he used the small joystick control to direct the light on the small craft. It was an open wooden skiff about sixteen feet long. How it was still floating was no small miracle, because the small boat looked like it had been through a sea battle.

"Morgan, are there people in that boat?"

Chapter 4

MORGAN YANKED THE LEVER, shifting the boat into neutral, grabbed the ship's phone, and hit the ship-wide button.

"Water Horse, Water Horse, we have people in the water in a small skiff off our starboard bow. All hands to the aft deck for recovery and rescue. Jerry, bring the med kit."

I grabbed a portable spotlight out of the cabinet below the nav station and shot out of the pilothouse to the side deck. I pointed the spotlight on the small boat as it came closer to our bow. Morgan would maneuver *Water Horse* so the skiff would slip down the starboard side of our hull for recovery. I followed the boat with the light as it drifted down the length of our deck, and now I could see that the passengers were actually one human and a large dog. The skiff came alongside the aft deck and Beau snagged the gunnel with a boathook, guiding it toward the boarding platform on the starboard stern. A damaged line cleat remained on the skiff's gunnel amidship, and Beau looped a line around it as Jas made the other end fast to a cleat on *Water Horse*.

Jerry joined Beau on the platform, stepped over into the skiff, and pulled a towel off what we could now see was a male, maybe in his twenties. Jerry checked for a pulse. "He's alive, but just barely. Let's get him to one of the guest cabins. Jas, pull me a saline drip from the med cooler. Beau, I'm going to hand him over to you."

Jerry picked the young, emaciated man up gently in his arms. He passed him to Beau, who easily climbed the steps back to the aft deck and headed directly through the rear cabin hatch to one of our guest cabins. Jerry then turned to the big gray shaggy dog that was as emaciated as the man. The dog's eyes were open, but he didn't try to move. Jerry knelt and gave the dog a gently stroke across his head.

"Hey there, big boy, what's your story?"

The dog looked up at Jerry, and although he wasn't able to move, the poor pup was able to give the slightest wag from the tip of his tail. Rudy stepped up to the aft rail and down the steps to the platform. He pushed Jas and me out of the way and said, "Jerry, hand him up to me. I'll take care of him."

Rudy had a blanket over his shoulder, and as Jerry gathered the large but clearly starved animal in his arms, Rudy unfolded the blanket and carefully wrapped the gangly gray-haired dog in the army-green wool and turned to start back up the stairs. Jas and I reached to give him a hand since his arms were so full of dog and Rudy snapped, totally out of character.

"I got him! I got him! I'll take him to the shop."

Jas and I looked at each other, a little taken aback, and Rudy disappeared through the aft hatch. The work light on the stern lit the area up well, and it was now easy to get a good look at the skiff. It had been through hell, with large chunks missing from the gunnels and topsides. There was evidence of an outboard motor at one time, but only part of the bracket remained, along with a section of engine cowling lying on the floor of the skiff. It looked like another section of the topsides had bullet holes across much of it. What had this poor guy stumbled into?

Turning up to Jas, I said. "Let's lift the skiff up on deck."

"You got it. Rig a couple of lines and I'll get the boom ready."

With the line Beau had used to tie the boat off, along with one other, I fashioned two lifting points for the boom. The skiff was not heavy and the lines were plenty strong to lift the small boat up onto the deck. Jas swung the boom over and above my position as the lifting hook lowered within reach. I attached the hook to the lifting loop and spun my index finger in the air, signaling Jas to lift away. As the skiff lifted from the water, I easily guided it up and over the rail and Jas lowered it to the deck. Once off the platform, I crossed the work area and picked up a ship phone mounted to the cabin bulkhead and rang the pilothouse.

"Pilothouse."

"Morgan, we've taken on one male passenger, alive, but very weak. Beau has taken him to a guest cabin and Jerry is going to start an IV. We've also taken on a dog."

"A dog?"

"Yeah, and our chief engineer has, in no certain terms, taken charge over—it. Let's call Mexico Maritime Search and Rescue, and apprise them of our situation, and we'll update them as soon as Jerry can make a better assessment."

"Roger that," Morgan answered. "I'll point us toward Cancun and take us to full cruise."

In the guest cabin, the man was still unconscious as Jerry checked his vitals.

"He's really weak," Jerry said, listening to the man's heart through his stethoscope. "I'd like to see if the saline helps before I try anything else. It's clear he's suffering from exposure and dehydration, but Michael, he's got two gunshot wounds as well."

Jerry pulled back the sheet, revealing a deep graze through the very top of the man's left shoulder and another on the edge of his right calf. My chest tightened and my past experiences as a war zone videographer began pulling and scratching at an old emotional wound, trying to reopen it. Horrific sights in Somalia, Afghanistan, the wartime destruction in Iraq, and then there was South Sudan, where everything changed for me. Seeing innocent people hurt needlessly still had a profound and powerful grip on me, and I knew it always would.

The man stirred slightly, and his eyes weakly blinked open. Jerry leaned closer to the man and said in Spanish, "My name is Jerry. What's your name?"

The barely conscious patient managed to whisper "Alejandro" hoarsely.

"Alejandro, we've called the Coast Guard. We're going to get help for you. Can you tell me where you are from?"

Alejandro's eyes grew heavy again, and I thought we'd lose him, but he whispered, "Fishing, out of San Crisanto," and then his eyes closed, unconscious.

I pulled out my phone and opened the navigation app to look at the Yucatán Peninsula on the small chart. Zooming in, I found San Crisanto; it was halfway across the east–west coast of the Yucatán. If this man were fishing off the coast of that town and something happened, he had drifted hundreds of miles and may have been adrift for days. No wonder he was in such terrible shape.

Entering the pilothouse, I found Morgan on the radio with Mexico's Maritime SAR. From the radio chatter, it was clear they were sending a rescue chopper to our location from the Mexican naval base in Puerto Morelos, just over a hundred miles away. Morgan was relaying our position, course, and speed to the dispatcher, as well as receiving instructions for getting the rescue crew safely on deck. When Morgan completed the call, he said, "Let's get radios on everyone and then patch Jerry straight in to the medics on the chopper for vitals on our castaway."

"On it," I said as I picked up three radios, tossing one to Morgan. "The guy's vitals are very weak, and he has two nonfatal gunshots wounds."

"Gunshot wounds? Did he say anything about what happened?"

"He managed to say he was from San Crisanto, but that was it."

"San Crisanto? Isn't that way down the coast to the west?" Morgan asked.

"Yeah, this guy may have been drifting a long time. The boat looks like it's taken some gunfire."

"Well, can't say that I'm shocked. There are big boy bad guys in these waters. Drugs, smuggling, and human trafficking."

"He's just a young kid. I guess he could be up to no good, but you don't meet many bad guys that take their dog along," I said.

"Yeah, what's up with the dog?" Morgan asked.

"Rudy got one look at the mutt and swooped in like a mother bear. I've never seen him like that. He's down in the shop patching him up, I think. I'll check on him after we get this guy loaded on the chopper. I'm going to run a radio down to Jerry. Ship-wide hail Beau and Jas and have them pick up radios from the camera shop and brief them on the inbound chopper."

"Will do."

Back down in the guest cabin, Jerry was hanging another bag of saline into Alejandro's IV. He was still unconscious and his color hadn't improved. As I got closer to the bed, I handed Jerry a radio. "A rescue chopper is coming in from Puerto Morelos."

"Good thing. His pulse is weaker, and he started running a fever," Jerry said.

"Has he come around again?"

"No, nothing since you left."

"Morgan is going to patch you in with the medic on the

chopper for some vitals. Sounds like they'll be to us in less than thirty minutes."

"Roger that," Jerry said.

Back on the aft deck, Jas and Beau were preparing for the arrival of the rescue team. They placed LED-lit cones in a large circle around the open area on the work deck and cleared away any other equipment. Within minutes, I could hear the heavy thumping of the rotors from the approaching rescue helicopter. We tuned our radios to the emergency VHF frequency so we could all hear the instructions from the chopper crew. Over the radio, the pilot talked us through each step of the process in English, before one of the rescue crew dropped a guideline down to our work deck. I picked up and firmed the line to assist his descent and the chopper's winch began slowly lowering a man down to us. Moments later, his feet touched down on the deck, followed by a bas-ket-type stretcher. Once the man gave the chopper the all clear, it rose, pulling away from its position directly over us, and we escorted the navy rescue swimmer to the guest cabin where Jerry prepared our patient for transport.

Stepping into the cabin, the navy corporal extended his hand to Jerry and said in accented English, "Corporal Navarro. Can you bring me up to speed since our last vital check?"

Jerry wasted no time. "BP ninety over sixty-two, pulse

fifty-one, and blood-ox is eighty-eight. I've dropped two bags of saline and nothing else."

The medic pulled his own med kit from his back and began rechecking Alejandro's vitals, and nodded as he listened to Jerry's report. "Was he conscious at all?"

"He came around briefly and told us his name was Alejandro and that he was from San Crisanto," Jerry answered.

Examining the gunshot wound on the man's shoulder, the corporal asked, "Did he give any indication of what happened out there?"

"No," I said. "But looks like his skiff was shot up pretty bad."

Corporal Navarro's eyebrow raised as he continued checking Alejandro's condition and looking at the second gunshot wound on the calf. "These are definitely gunshots."

"The skiff is sitting out on our deck. We can drop it off in Cancun when we arrive, if you think it will be helpful in any investigation," I said.

"I'll run it up the chain," the corporal said as he began packing up his equipment.

Jas and Beau brought the stretcher into the cramped space and we all worked together to load Alejandro into the basket with Corporal Navarro's instruction. On our way back out to the lift zone, the corporal radioed the chopper to get into position for the hoist. Out on deck, Navarro stepped over to the

skiff and looked at the damage and turned back to me, shout-
ing over the rotor wash. "You are right! Our commanders
back at Morelos will want to see this."

I handed the corporal a business card, and he read it, then
shouted, "Nice to meet you, Captain Gannon. My comman-
der will reach out!"

"There's one more thing," I shouted. "The man had a dog
with him!"

"A dog?" he asked.

I nodded.

"We can't take a dog, Captain!"

"No problem! Our engineer is taking care of it."

"I probably shouldn't say this, but the man is very weak,
and it does not look good."

"Understood. I know you and your team will do your
best," I said.

With that, Navarro got the lines secured for the hoist and
as fast as he appeared, the navy corporal followed the basket
up and into the side door of the powerful craft and the chest
rattling thump of the chopper faded into the star-filled sky.

Things can go from peaceful to heart-pounding terror on
the water in the blink of an eye. And now, after the last
adrenaline filled ninety minutes, a few seconds passed, and it
was once again strangely peaceful out on deck, under the
stars. But my gut told me it'd probably not stay that way.

Chapter 5

As I stepped into the shop adjacent to the engine room, I found Rudy on his knees feeding his furry charge with what looked like a turkey baster.

"How's the patient?"

"He's weak, Michael. I've gotten a little bone broth into him, but he's in bad shape."

"You seemed a little agitated out on deck. Anything else going on?"

Rudy looked down, a little embarrassed. "I'm sorry about that. Seeing those two adrift and starving made my way-back machine start misfiring."

"Anything you'd like to talk about?"

"Ahh, it was a long time ago. I was just a kid."

"Some of the things we go through, we carry with us every day, and even though time softens the rough edges, it keeps a pretty good grip on us."

Rudy looked down at the dog and patted his head, and said, "I was twenty-one years old and fresh off the farm in Idaho. I'd seen enough potato fields and flat plains to last a lifetime. So on my eighteenth birthday, I joined the merchant marines with my buddy Eddie Harper. Eddie and I had gone to school together since the third grade." Rudy paused, then laughed a little. "They called him Spud. We both came from potato country, but for some reason, he got stuck with the name, and he never seemed to mind. Anyway, we went through training together, and, by pure luck, we both got assigned to our first ship together, a freighter called the *Marisol Trader*. The ocean grabbed hold of me in a profound way. After my first month at sea, I knew it would be home for the rest of my life. We'd only been on the job for six months and were off the coast of Northern Africa, headed for Lisbon, Portugal, when pirates boarded our ship before dawn. They shot and killed the first officer. Then they beat the captain badly. We were a small crew, only eighteen. They roughed up the rest of us, and Eddie took a rifle butt to the head. They took anything valuable we had, which wasn't much, and started loading us into the lifeboats. It was a Tuesday about nine a.m., when they left us adrift. I still don't know how, but Eddie and I ended up in a boat by ourselves and we drifted out there for eleven days."

"Eleven days!" I said. "No food or no water?"

"There was a little emergency water in the lifeboat that lasted three days, but then nothing. I managed to catch a little evaporated water with a small tarp, but it wasn't enough for both of us. Eddie started getting sick on the sixth day and on the evening of the eighth day, he went to sleep . . . and never woke up. I'd pretty much given up when this old fishing scow found us and took us aboard on the eleventh day. I woke up two days later in a hospital in Morocco." Rudy starred off distantly for a few seconds before saying, "Making that call to Eddie's folks was the hardest thing I've ever done."

"Rudy, I'm so sorry, I had no idea."

"It was a long time ago, and there's been a lot of water under the keel since then. But seeing that skiff all shot up and ghosting along, kinda brought it all back."

"That's understandable."

"I'll tell you this, Michael. If anyone ever tries to board this boat, I will fight till my last breath before I give way to a pirate ever again."

"And I promise that you'll never make that fight alone."

Rudy nodded his understanding and reached to give the dog another taste of the broth.

"What kind of dog is he . . . or she?" I asked.

"It's a he. And he looks like a Scottish deerhound, but I'm not sure what a deerhound is doing off the coast of Mexico."

The dog managed to raise his head with a little more energy as he licked at the turkey baster full of broth.

"I'll get him cleaned up and on his feet, and see if I can find a shelter for him in Cancun," Rudy said, sounding a little resigned to what he believed we'd expect him to do.

"You know, it might not be so bad having him aboard. Would you mind caring for him until his owner can take him back?"

Rudy's eyes brightened. "Ya think?" He covered his excitement with a more serious face. "I mean, there's a lot to do getting the boat ready for this assignment and we'll have a new guest aboard soon. But I think I can keep him out of the way and I don't mind the extra responsibility."

"We'll all pitch in," I said. "If he's a member of the crew, he's a member of the crew and part of the team. He doesn't have a tag and his owner wasn't able to tell us his name. What do you think we should call him?"

Rudy stroked the dog's head, and the affection seemed appreciated. After a thoughtful pause, Rudy said, "I think I'll call him Harper after my buddy Eddie. What ya think about that, boy? You okay if we call you Harper?"

The dog licked Rudy's hand and his tail wagged, thumping the deck. I bent down and gave our newest crew member a pat on the head. "Well, all right. Harper it is," I said. "I'm going to go relieve Morgan at the helm. We should be in Cancun late tomorrow afternoon."

"Roger that, Michael. I'll have Harper here, all cleaned up, and smelling better before our guest arrives."

Once in the pilothouse, Morgan gave a big stretch. "Just in time. Even with all the excitement, that big dinner has me ready for a nap."

"Sorry, your dinner was probably cold," I said.

"Well, I was able to stop just shy of licking the plate."

"Go get some rack time, and I'll see you in the morning."

"Oh, what's up with the dog?" Morgan asked.

"That would be Harper."

"He's already got a name?"

"He's going to be part of the crew until his owner can take him back. Rudy downplayed it, but he seems like a boy with a new puppy. He told me a story about a run-in he had with pirates in his early years as a merchant marine. Pretty scary stuff. He was adrift for eleven days and lost a good friend."

Morgan was quiet for a second and said, "An experience like that changes a man, even a tough SOB like Rudy. You stay on the ocean as long as him and you see and experience some stuff for sure. I'm damn glad he's on our side."

"Me too."

"I'll see you in the morning." And Morgan left me in the pilothouse with the moonlight and a quiet sea.

The rear pilothouse door opened. "Well, that was crazy!" Ellie said, as she broke the brief peace at the helm. "Are you guys magnets for this kinda stuff or what?"

I chuckled. "We don't go looking for it, but some of these things do seem to find us."

"It didn't seem like that man was doing so well when they loaded him in the helicopter," Ellie said.

"No, he was very weak."

"And Rudy is taking care of the dog?"

"He is," I said.

"I wish I didn't have to go home tomorrow. It's so beautiful here."

"If we find anything unusual down here, think you could help us out?" I asked.

"Are you kidding me? I'm set on go. I've already been doing research on Bermeja and the earlier surveys to find the island."

"That doesn't surprise me at all."

"One island missing. Maybe it's nature. Two islands missing, I smell something rotten."

"Maybe," I said. "But charting errors were common before GPS and satellite technology became common, and the

Gulf is a moving, changing, living thing. Wind and storms alter this body of water and coastline every day."

"If there's anything here, Michael, I want in. You hear me?"

"I got you, sis. You want to sit with me a while?"

"Yeah, I'm still too ramped up to sleep."

I pulled up an additional helm seat and locked it in place with the safety latches on the deck. Ellie and I sat there, mostly in silence, and watched the stars track across the clear sky as the bow of *Water Horse* cut through the silvery water, steaming us closer to our temporary stop in one of Mexico's most popular tropical playgrounds.

Ellie finally broke the silence. "I can see why you love it out here. You're a different person when you're out here on the water, Michael."

"I do love it. But what do you mean, different?"

"I don't know. A look in your eyes, an easiness to you, that I don't see when we're back home."

"But I love the Low Country," I said.

"I know you do. And you love your family, but you're still different"—she waved her hand out at the darkness that surrounded us—"out here."

I didn't know how to reply, so I sat silently looking through the pilothouse windows at the moon reflecting off the water. Ellie stood, yawned, and stretched.

"I'm hitting the sack." She stepped over to me and patted me on the cheek. "I'll leave you with your mistress. But remember, my dear brother, it may be lonely growing old with only a boat and the ocean." And with that, she was off.

Now why did she have to go and say that?

What would have been a peaceful watch, would now be filled with mental macerations about things I had put in the "for later" box. She's always been able to read me like a book. Morgan's exterior was a little more immune to Ellie's physiological prodding, but she had always been able to push my buttons, and oftentimes, she was annoyingly right.

The next several watch changes passed without incident, and the next day was a beautiful carbon copy of the day before, with sunny skies, seventy-two degrees, and calm seas. At three p.m., we were twelve miles off the harbor entrance of BrisaMar Marina, north and east of the city center of Cancun. We made an effortless ten knots westward as the coast of the Yucatán first appeared as tiny bumps on the far horizon.

Morgan was back at the helm and Rudy was below, nursing our new hound, who had made impressive progress overnight. When I checked on the pair after breakfast, Harper was sitting up and panting happily as Rudy doted on him. Everyone else was out on deck soaking up the day, especially Ellie. She stood on the bow, putting as much sunshine as she could fit in her pockets before boarding the plane that would return her to the gray winter of New York City in December.

With the weather and sea state being so calm, we had set up a few folding chairs on the bow, just forward of the cabin house. I sat in one, enjoying a large glass of iced tea and watching a grouping of four flying fish as they sprang out of the water, glided for several yards above the surface, and dipped back into the turquoise water. Jas plopped down into the empty seat next to me.

"Rudy is already crazy about Harper. He's like a new mother. I don't think I've ever seen this side of him."

"I think he's doing more than just taking care of a dog," I said.

Jas turned and raised an eyebrow at me, waiting for an answer. "He'll tell you when he's ready."

"Well, I like him too. It'll be hard to give him back."

"I didn't realize you were such a big dog lover," I said.

Jas punched me in the arm. "I love dogs! My dad always said, 'never trust a man that doesn't like dogs.'"

Rubbing my arm, I said, "Damn! Hey, I love dogs too. I just didn't know that about you."

With what seemed like the slightest hint of regret, Jas said, "Well . . . good. You know, Harper should stay with us until Alejandro can care for him again."

"Of course. We'll know more when we check on his status with search and rescue. I'll reach out to them after we tie up this afternoon."

As we got closer to shore, the pleasure boat traffic increased, and watercraft of every kind zipped back and forth across our path. We had to keep a close watch on most of these "captains," where a set of keys and bottle of sunscreen comprised their entire skill set in navigating an active waterway. I joined Morgan in the pilothouse to lend him an extra set of eyes as we threaded our way through the chaos and put our bow into the entrance channel of BrisaMar Marina.

I radioed the harbormaster, and he gave us docking instructions for a long, side-tie pier, out on the far edge of the harbor. The docks and facilities appeared maintained and well-equipped, but this was not a pleasure boat marina. Work boats, commercial fishing boats, and barges filled the docks and large repair yard. As we approached our assigned dock space, it appeared we already had company awaiting our arrival. Eight Mexican Navy personnel carrying rifles stood on the pier, looking impatient. Morgan expertly brought us alongside the dock and the crew went to work dropping fenders. Despite their stern looks, the navy men took our dock lines and helped us secure *Water Horse* in her temporary berth.

I descended to the main deck to greet the sailors, and one man stepped forward.

"Hola, *Water Horse*, I am Petty Officer Morales. May I speak with Captain Gannon, por favor?"

I stepped over onto the dock and extended my hand. "I'm Captain Gannon. Nice to meet you, Petty Officer Morales."

"Captain, I understand you are in possession of the boat where the man was found adrift."

"We are, Petty Officer. It's stowed on our stern deck. You are welcome to come aboard and inspect the skiff."

The petty officer nodded and he and his men stepped aboard and I led them back to the aft deck where the skiff sat on its bottom. Morales walked around the shot up open hull for several minutes, making verbal notes in Spanish to one of the other sailors that busily recorded them in a small notebook he retrieved from his shirt pocket.

"Captain Gannon, did the man you found indicate what kind of trouble he encountered?"

"He did not. He told us his name was Alejandro and was fishing out of San Crisanto. Then he lost consciousness and stayed that way until your SAR team lifted him up to the chopper. How is Alejandro?"

The petty officer looked down and shook his head. When he looked back up at me, he said, "His name was Alejandro García. He was twenty-two years old. . . . He passed away this morning."

I wasn't surprised to hear the news, but I had been hopeful for a different outcome. "We're sorry to hear that, Petty Officer. Did he have a family?"

"He leaves behind his mother and a younger sister," Morales said.

"I assume you don't have any idea what happened out there?" I asked.

"No more than you. This is the second similar incident in the last six months. We fight against the narcos and smugglers, but the Gulf is a big body of water. But we will continue to investigate."

"Please extend our condolences to the family," I said.

"Indeed, I will, Captain."

"Were you aware that he had a dog with him?" I asked.

"A dog?"

"Yes, a large dog."

The petty officer scratched his chin in thought. "Captain, this is a poor family. Another mouth to feed is not ideal with the loss of Alejandro. Is there any way that, perhaps . . ."

Over the petty officer's shoulder, I could see Rudy standing halfway through one of the aft cabin hatches observing our conversation while wiping a wrench clean with a shop rag.

"If it's okay with the family, we'll be glad to take care of the dog, Petty Officer Morales."

Rudy looked away and quickly disappeared back into the cabin.

"That would be very satisfactory, Captain, gracias."

Smiling, I said, "Our ship's engineer has developed a strong fondness for the dog in a short time, so he will take good care of him. Would you like us to lift the skiff off and onto the dock for you?"

"That would be very helpful. But, Captain, would you mind telling me what you and your team are working on here in Mexican waters?"

I kept it vague, but I didn't want to start our trip on the wrong side of the Mexican Navy. "We'll be escorting a scientist from your government for some survey work."

A broad grin spread across the petty officer's face. "Ahh, more searching for Bermeja, I suspect."

I pasted on my best "guilty feigning innocent" confused teen expression, but he wasn't buying. "We haven't received a full briefing yet. We're to take a Dr. Cruz aboard this afternoon."

"Yes. Dr. Cruz. He is quite respected."

"We look forward to helping any way we can," I said.

He extended his hand. "Happy hunting, Captain."

I shook hands with the petty officer and left Beau and Jerry in charge of off-loading the skiff, and headed to the shop to give Rudy the news.

As I stepped into the shop, I hardly recognized the clean, handsome canine that sat up next to Rudy's workbench. His previously long dirty, matted gray coat was now clean and brushed, almost shiny. Rudy knelt in front of the dog, scratching him behind an ear, speaking gently, as if delivering difficult news to a good friend. I gave them a moment and said, "You got the drift of all that up on deck, I assume?"

"I did. I was just bringing Harper up to speed."

"Well, is he going to sign on with us?"

Rudy stood up with a big smile. "What say you, Harper, want to become a crew member aboard *Water Horse*?"

A few short pants and a deep "woof" filled the small space.

"I think he's in, Captain."

Chapter 6

Standing in the galley, I briefed Jas, Beau, and Jerry on my conversation with Petty Officer Morales. "I'm afraid Alejandro passed away this morning. There were just too many things working against him by the time we found him."

The three received the news in somber silence with lowered heads.

"Certainly seems like someone unleashed hell on them in the skiff," Jerry said.

"The petty officer mentioned fishermen and tourists have run-ins with the narcos from time to time, but this is the second incident in six months," I said.

Beau shook his head. "Shooting up a skiff with an unarmed man and his dog is damned brutal."

"They better hope Rudy never finds them," Jas said, and we all laughed.

"Okay, let's get the boat cleaned up and ready to receive Dr. Cruz. He'll be arriving in an hour. Jerry, let's bunk him in the VIP cabin. And Jas, Dr. Cruz will have some equipment, so will you set up the lab space next to the camera shop so he can work?"

"You got it, Cap," Jas said, with Jerry also nodding yes to his instructions.

"Beau, he'll also have some dive and other equipment. Let's prepare a locker for him on the work deck and help him get squared away out there."

Beau was a great utility man. He could do a little of everything and all of it well. He kept our decks and working spaces in tip-top shape and had shown himself to be a great resource for Rudy on ship systems and Jas and Morgan on more tech-related issues. Beau was originally part of our last client's crew with the Sea Watcher team. He just fit in so well with the Water Horse family that at the end of the mission I asked Sea Watchers' Kyle Bennett for permission to offer him a full-time spot aboard our boat, and I was so glad he accepted.

"Understood," Beau answered.

With that, the crew quietly dispersed to get to work. I looked up to see Ellie step into the galley with her bag packed, ready to go. She stood quietly until the galley had cleared and looked up to meet my eyes. "I heard the news. I am sorry to hear that. Want me to get the address for the family and send something on Water Horse's behalf?"

"That'd be very nice of you, sis. Thank you."

"No problem. I'm assuming Rudy already has Harper fetching tools."

I laughed. "Almost! So, this is you headed to NYC?"

"I'm on the seven p.m. flight. I called a cab. It should be here anytime."

Morgan stepped into the galley just in time for goodbyes. "You pack light, sis."

"Shorts, T-shirts, and a bathing suit don't take up very much room. Although the ride from the airport to my apartment will be an adventure, it's supposed to be thirty-four degrees there. But I'll reaccept winter—tomorrow."

"Good strategy," Morgan said.

"If you guys find anything . . . hinky, you'll call, right?"

"Yes," I said. "Come on, we'll walk you out."

"Michael, remember what I said last night, okay?"

I ignored the comment and led her through the hatch. Morgan gave me a look, but in a rare display of restraint, he let it go.

The three of us headed for the main deck. As Morgan and I followed Ellie down the starboard side to the boarding steps, a truck pulled up next to an awaiting cab, and Dr. Mateo Cruz stepped out. His bronzed biceps stretched the sleeves of a brightly colored golf shirt, and his shoulder-length black curly hair stood in perfect contrast to a million-dollar smile, beacon bright, in the late afternoon sun. He waved enthusiastically. "Hola, Captain Gannon!"

"Hola, Dr. Cruz," I answered.

Ellie turned back to me and said, "I knew I was leaving too soon."

Morgan, sounding a little protective, said, "You're leaving just in time."

Ellie smacked him on the arm. "I love you both. Be careful . . . and call me!"

"We love you too," I said.

Jas stepped up behind me and said softly, "Wow, that's our guest, huh? I'll help him get his gear on board."

"Beau's helping him get settled," I said a little too quickly.

Jas flashed her mischievous smile. "Roger that, Captain," and she spun and headed back to the lab space.

"Subtle," Morgan said.

"Shut up. Let's go greet our marine geologist."

"Permission to come aboard, Captain?" Dr. Cruz said from the dock.

"Permission granted," I said.

The scientist came aboard and extended his hand. "Good to see you, Captain. It looks like we have beautiful weather to begin our adventure, yes?"

"Dr. Cruz, this is my partner and brother, Morgan Gannon."

"Very pleased to meet you, Morgan. Please call me Mateo," he said, extending his hand.

"Good to meet you, Mateo. Welcome aboard the *Water Horse*. We'll have you squared away in no time."

"Gracias. I was hoping you would allow me to take you and your crew to dinner this evening before we begin our work. I know the perfect place."

"That's very kind of you. The crew's been aboard for a few weeks now, so an evening ashore would be appreciated. Thank you, Dr. Cruz," I said.

Patting me on the shoulder like we were old friends, the doctor said, "Captain, please call me Mateo."

"Thank you, Mateo. We'll get your gear stowed and take you up on that dinner."

"Excellent," Mateo said, his blinding grin in full effect.

Ninety minutes later, our crew mustered on the dock and I introduced Mateo to the team. He greeted everyone individually with exuberant grins and hand-pumping.

"Very good, my new friends. Now, let us share cold cerveza and a good meal before we strike out tomorrow."

The smiling pied-piper led our team several blocks to a well-worn waterfront bar, with graffiti covering the cracked stucco walls and lit only with worn neon lights. Music poured out of the open windows and doors. It was clearly a local spot, which we normally love. But in Mexico, good judgment might lead you to keep walking right past this one.

"You carrying?" I asked Morgan.

"You wearing pants?" he answered. And I snickered.

"Well, it does have windows," Morgan whispered as we approached.

One of our unwritten rules was to avoid establishments without windows. No windows in a bar was usually a bad sign. We had another rule to steer clear of establishments that promoted driving the motorcycles . . . directly into the bar.

"The Marinero Salado is a place where men of the sea drink and eat," Mateo said proudly, as if he were an old mariner himself. And maybe he was—but he didn't look like one. "The cervezas are ice cold and the fish is excelente."

We entered, and Mateo greeted the bartender as if he was a regular. He made a request in Spanish, and the bartender pointed to a large table in the back of the room. A server came around the side of the bar and got us settled around the large rectangular table and took our drink orders. Our beers arrived, and the conversation was light as Mateo Cruz smiled and intentionally engaged the team.

Halfway through my second beer, I heard a loud voice in English call over the noise of the crowd and music. "MG! Is that you?"

Morgan turned and stood. "Sims Mitchell! Is there any way possible that you've actually gotten bigger?"

The man was a walking mountain. He had to have stood six-five or six-six. His shaggy blond hair gave him a surfer vibe, but his body screamed Dwayne "The Rock" Johnson. I stood up next to Morgan as the man approached, getting bigger all the time. He pulled Morgan into a big bear hug, lifting him off his feet. "MG, man! It's been a while, brother."

"Sims, this is my twin brother, Michael."

Sims shot out his freakishly large hand. "Michael, I've heard a lot about you. Good to finally meet you."

"What the hell you doing in this hole in the wall?" Sims asked Morgan.

"I'm working with Michael now, aboard his research vessel, *Water Horse*. We're doing some survey work in the area."

"I wondered where you landed when you left the Teams. That's great."

"How about you?" Morgan asked.

"Left the Teams last year. I hunted and fished a few months and then I missed the life, so I signed on with a personal security firm based out of Miami. For the last six months, I've been working security on a superyacht owned by a company out of Austin. The money is insane and I love the water."

"Good for you, Sims. Can I buy you a beer?"

"Always," Sims said, as he pulled up an empty chair from an adjoining table. But when he sat, he looked like a grown-up sitting in a kid's school chair from a first-grade classroom. Beers arrived and Sims asked, "What kinda surveying are you guys doing down here?"

I leaned forward to offer a nonanswer, but Morgan beat me to the punch.

"Pretty routine, the Commission of Aquaculture and Fisheries wanted a survey of sport fish populations off the Yucatán, so they could determine if they needed to charge more fees for gringos to come down and fish."

It was an excellent answer. I was impressed.

"Well, counting fish in the Gulf of Mexico beats running around in the sandbox, or getting shot at by warlords," Sims said.

"Yeah, it's not bad, and Michael only rides my ass about half as much as Captain Simpson."

We all laughed, and Sims reached over with his bottle, offering me a toast.

"What about your gig?" Morgan asked.

"Run of the mill rich parties and client entertaining, down here, out of sight and out of mind. The client wants a discreet playground for his three-hundred-eighty-foot yacht, with no reporters or 'lookie-loos.'"

"Roger that," Morgan said. "You look good. The tropics agree with you."

"Shit, brother, it all looks good on me."

We all laughed again, but I suspected he was right. Sims was a specimen right out of a movie. He looked down the long table at Mateo, who had quickly become the center of attention.

"Who's the guy with the teeth?"

"He's just our client ride-along," I answered.

"Personable fella. Government official?"

"Low level director. I think he's someone's nephew," Morgan answered.

Sims laughed and shook his head. "Isn't it always the case."

A commotion broke out near the bar. A small shoving match between two fishermen wasn't attracting much attention until a more aggressive shove pushed one of the men crashing into Sims, knocking his beer to the floor. Moving faster than anyone that big should move, Sims stood and grabbed the man around the throat with his left hand. The man clawed at Sims's hand, but it was like a small animal struggling against a steel trap, and within seconds, the smaller man looked like a paralyzed kitten being carried by the scruff of the neck. Sims cocked his massive right arm with a clinched anvil of a fist attached to the end. Morgan barked out his name with an intensity used to snap a recruit to attention. "Sergeant MITCHELL!"

The giant registered the tone of voice like a prepro-grammed machine. His face completely changed, as if coming back into consciousness. He released the man, who now stood staring up at Sims like a mouse just released from the claw of an eagle. The man who started all the shoving, along with ev-ery other customer, stood silent and still.

"Why don't you men take this matter outside, immedi-ately after bringing me a fresh beer," Sims's low baritone voice now had a surprisingly friendly tone. The man stand-ing in front of Sims nodded eagerly and backed up toward the bar. Sims turned to us and sat, smiling. "Sorry about that. Old instincts die hard."

"Roger that, big man," Morgan said and took a tug off his beer.

The crowd noise resumed and the room's energy normalized.

"Hey, you remember that time in Caracas?" Sims asked. "I thought for sure we'd end up in a nasty holding cell after that night."

"Yeah, we . . . or mostly you, tried to tear the whole bar apart," Morgan said.

"As I recall, it was you, MG, that threw the owner through the front window."

"Because he was about to crack your enormous head with a ball bat. There, Tiny."

"Oh man, good times."

"Oh yeah, good times." Morgan laughed.

"Don't you ever miss it?" Sims asked.

Morgan was quiet for a second before saying, "I miss the brotherhood the most. There's nothing else like the brotherhood in the Teams. Just knowing that group of men had your back, no matter how 'to shit' a situation turned. There's nothing like it. I don't miss having to always break stuff and tear things down in the name of good. I know it's a job that must be done and I know what we did was important. We saved a lot of lives. But man, seems like we always had to use a sledgehammer to do it. Now working with Michael, I feel like we have a chance to . . . just do some good."

Morgan had never said anything like that to me before. I knew his time on the Teams was very important to him, but I'd never heard him express it that way.

Sims sat listening to Morgan and then burst out laughing. "Damn, MG, you've gone all Socrates on me!"

Morgan broke the moment as he laughed along with the big man. The two former teammates fell back into more old mission stories and told each other about team members that had either seen or heard from in the last few years. As the laughter faded, Sims nodded and took the last swig of his beer and stood. Damn, he was big.

"Well, boys, I'm going to leave it with you. I've gotta get back to the boat. We're headed further west, down the peninsula. Michael, it was good to meet you."

I stood to shake his hand. "Good to meet you too, Sims. Fair winds to you."

"MG, great to see you, brother."

"You too, Sims. Be good, yeah?"

"Nah, I'll just be good at it."

The two former teammates hugged, and the crowd noticeably split as the Goliath made his way toward the exit.

We sat quietly for a moment and I could tell Morgan was thinking about his more philosophical moment with Sims. "So, what's the story with him?" I asked.

"Good operator, and overall good guy. He likes shiny things, so he was always looking for the side hustle. Never anything that crossed the line, but his toes got close a few times. I always trusted him to have my back in a fight, but off duty, I kept a little distance between us. Without the code of the Teams, I was never sure how he'd behave out here in the wild."

"He's a bruiser, that's for sure."

"Yeah, and freakishly strong. I've seen guys his size

dropped like third period French, but I never saw anyone best Sims."

"Good information to have," I said. "Anything else on your mind? Your forehead has that wrinkle thing going."

"That's usually your fault," Morgan said. "No, just wondering what the chances were that Sims would run into me in this unlikely little establishment. His boat is no doubt docked in a nicer part of town."

"I don't know about that. You and I would look for a local spot like this instead of drinking at the executive club."

"Yeah, but we're not Sims," Morgan said, and took a thoughtful swallow of beer.

Food came along with fresh beers. It was fresh, spicy, and delicious. The crew was enjoying themselves and you could feel the energy at the table recharge the batteries of our team. I glanced down at the far end of the table where Mateo appeared to be telling Jas a story that involved lots of animated arm movements and theatrical facial expressions. Jas sat captivated, listening earnestly as she smiled in that way that . . . well that way she does. I caught myself clinching the sides of my chair, like I wanted to rip the edges of the seat off, and it surprised me. Morgan noticed my expression. "Speaking of wrinkled foreheads, what's going on in that birdcage of yours?"

"Nothing," I said as I released my clinched fists.

"Man, not only are you a softie, you're a bad liar."

"C'mon, she's a crew member. I just don't trust our new doctor friend yet."

"Ah-huh. Well, caution is a good thing. And we'll keep an eye on 'Mr. Bright Smile' for sure. But you've got some other stuff bouncing around in there."

"Drink your beer, you old squid."

Morgan laughed and took a long draw off his cold cerveza.

I looked around the table at the stacks of empty plates and rows of dead soldier beer bottles and stood. "Water Horse, let's raise a bottle to our host, Dr. Cruz, for an outstanding meal and well-deserved night ashore."

"Hear! Hear!" came the replies around the table.

"And let's raise one more to a fellow waterman, Alejandro García. May he be blessed with endless sunsets on calm seas in a better place."

"To Alejandro!" came the replies in a more somber tone than the first.

"Water Horse, we'll muster in the galley at oh seven hundred for a full brief with Dr. Cruz and cast off shortly thereafter."

With that, I gave Jerry Styles, our first officer, the nod to start herding our team toward the door. I approached Dr. Cruz for a handshake. "Thanks again, Mateo. This was really nice of you."

"Captain, it was my pleasure. Your crew is intelligent and very engaging. Señora Jas is particularly impressive."

The tension returned to my hands, but I smiled and said, "She is indeed. She's a very valuable member of the team."

The crew laughed and joked on the walk back, reveling in the afterglow of beer and a good meal. Rounding the last corner, *Water Horse* sat in her berth with the soft pale glow of her deck lights urging sleepy sailors into comfortable berths. At the top of the boarding steps leading onto the deck sat an upright menacing looking beast that left little doubt that he was all business.

"What's up with that, Rudy?"

"Beats me, Cap. I left him in the shop."

As we approached, I said, "Permission to come aboard, Harper?"

"Woof!" was followed by a rhythmic tail thumping on the steel deck. I looked at Rudy and he just smiled like a proud dad. With our sentry's permission, the crew ambled up the boarding steps.

As Rudy stepped aboard, Harper fell in behind him down the side deck. "See you boys in the morning."

Morgan and I were left standing alone on deck, and as he headed to his cabin, I said, "Hey, Morgan?"

"Yeah?"

"I know we're not the Teams, but I hope you know that I'll always have your back, no matter how bad it gets."

"Brother, it's one of the few things that helps me to sleep at night. See you in the morning."

And he turned and went up the steps to his cabin. I just stood there a minute, breathing in the cool salt air and smiled, not sure if I had ever been given a bigger compliment.

Chapter 7

I SLEPT RESTLESSLY. The images of the shot up skiff and of an emaciated Alejandro kept creeping into my dozing dreams. At five-thirty, I rolled out of my bunk and I took a hot shower. I started the large industrial coffee urn for the team, and as soon as enough had dripped into the reservoir, I poured a partial cup and took the steps to the pilothouse to watch the sunrise. Stepping up behind the helm, I looked out onto the bow deck to find I wasn't the first one up. Dr. Cruz was on deck, shirtless, methodically going through a kata from a form of martial art. His impressive, muscled arms and back glistened with sweat even in the early morning twilight. I would need to ease my apprehension of the good doctor if we were going to effectively operate on this assignment, so I set my mind for a clean start and decided to offer a fresh cup of *Water Horse* coffee to our guest as he finished his workout.

The sun had just peeked over the dark horizon with golden whispers of a beautiful day as I stepped out onto the bow deck with two fresh cups. I approached Dr. Cruz as he toweled off, taking in the first light of the morning.

"Buen día, Mateo. Can I offer you a hot cup of coffee?"

Mateo turned, a little startled. "Ahhh, good morning, Captain. Gracias. It appears we will have a glorious day to begin our voyage. Mornings like this on the Gulf are magical, don't you think?"

I handed Mateo his cup. "They are indeed. Warm morning sun on your face with the smell of the salt air can soothe the soul."

"Sí . . . sí, Captain. In your previous career, you witnessed many things, that all this . . . would be very healing, no?"

Again, I was a little taken aback at his knowledge of my background, but I let it go. "Yes, but I also learned that people will hurt each other everywhere, just like the young fisherman we found adrift."

"Ah, the young Alejandro, that news was very tragic. A dark ocean can bring dangerous situations."

"What do you think we'll find out here, Mateo?"

"Honestly, Michael, I'm not sure. Left as isolated incidents, the islands, the oil, the political gamesmanship, it all sounds like history. But wrap them all together and we get the possibility of something more."

"There's a lot of political pressure around our mission. Let's hope we aren't facing a dangerous situation ourselves."

"You and your brother Morgan are thoughtful . . . and careful men. You will navigate us through any rough waters we encounter."

"Do you anticipate rough waters, Dr. Cruz?"

After a thoughtful pause, Mateo's face lightened, and his electric grin widened. "No. I see with the coming of morning, a chance for a better day, yes?"

"Always," I said. "I'll let you get cleaned up, and we'll see you in the galley for the briefing. Glad to have you with us."

"Gracias, Captain, I'll be there."

At seven, the crew surrounded the large dining table. Rudy placed a large bowl of fresh scrambled eggs next to a heaping plate of bacon as the crew began passing and spooning. Harper sat stoically by the galley entrance with a look of anticipation tempered with discipline. Rudy split a strip of bacon from the plate and turned to Harper. "Harper, you have a salute for the captain?"

Harper raised his right paw up against his right ear. "At

ease, sailor," Rudy said and tossed him the bit of bacon that Harper easily caught and swallowed.

"We learned that just this morning," Rudy said.

"We're clearly all replaceable," Beau said to chuckles around the table.

Dr. Cruz entered the galley as the laughter subsided. "Good morning, shipmates. I'm glad to see such high spirits this morning."

Turning to Mateo, I said, "Dr. Cruz, I'll turn this over to you if we can eat while we brief."

"That would be fine, Captain."

He took a seat at the head of the table and Rudy put a plate in front of him, along with a fresh cup.

"As your good captain has probably informed you, this all started when our government attempted to reverify the location of the tiny island of Bermeja. This island would extend Mexican territorial waters approximately two hundred kilometers into the Gulf. Two different extensive survey trips resulted in no trace of an island that has appeared on Spanish and Mexican charts since the 1800s. This has now dramatically decreased our government's leverage into the Gulf for oil exploration. Seven months ago, a second island, oddly named Isla Escondida, also vanished. My government has asked for your help in determining whether these occurrences are natural in origin, or if there is . . . some other explanation."

"Doctor, can you tell us where Bermeja is supposed to be?" I asked.

"It was approximately two-hundred-two kilometers off the western corner of the Yucatán at 22°33′ north, 91°22′ west. My plan is for us to travel to that location and search for traces of the island. We will collect numerous bottom samples. We will repeat the process at the previously charted location of Isla Escondida."

"What kind of bottom samples?" Jas asked.

"Bottom samples in that part of the Gulf should be consistent as far as mineral composition. We'll see if there is any difference between the surrounding bottom and the bottom where the island is supposed to be."

"How about our operating depths?" Morgan asked.

"On the actual search coordinates, I think we'll be less than twenty meters. If we expand our search, I don't think we'll need samples from anything over twenty-five meters, even though we'll be on the edge of the Yucatán Shelf. What is your cruising speed, Captain?"

"Twelve knots," I said.

Dr. Cruz did some quick math in his head and said, "Bermeja's coordinates will be a twenty-one-hour run at that speed. I can feed you the exact coordinates for both islands before we cast off."

"That'll do," I said. "All right, team. Let's make preparations to shove off in one hour. That'll put us on the first search location near daybreak tomorrow."

Out on the main deck, last-minute preparations were underway with extra gear being stowed and provisions loaded. An unmarked dark blue pickup pulled up to the dock and Petty Officer Morales stepped out. A bit surprised and a bit not, I met him at the bottom of the boarding stairs. "Petty Officer Morales, good to see you—again."

"Buenos dias, Captain. It looks like you're about to shove off."

"Yes, sir. Very soon now."

"Captain, against my better judgment, I wanted to share some information with you."

"Why against your better judgment?" I asked.

"Captain Gannon, you are an outsider here. But my instincts tell me I can trust you."

"I'm listening."

"Early this morning, we received a report about a small diving charter that is missing. They were out of a harbor just east of San Bruno. There are six people aboard the *Coral Explorer*, and they should have been back in port thirty-six hours ago. This type of incident is not unheard of. Like I mentioned before, when the narcos are active, fisherman or divers can accidentally interrupt drop offs or deliveries and trouble follows. But with two events in thirty days, this . . . this feels different."

"Petty Officer Morales, why confide in me?"

"I've been patrolling these waters for twenty-five years. I've had dealings with every type of captain, sailor, and scoundrel you could imagine. You develop a sense of man while standing on their deck."

"Thank you, Petty Officer."

"If you are going to search for Bermeja, you will be operating in areas known to have elevated instances of questionable activity. Please use caution, Captain."

"Note taken, sir. We're always very careful. Both my brother and I have operated in troubled areas of the world, so we're cautious by nature."

"The politics around this Bermeja issue have been heated as well. One of the ministers even accused your CIA of blowing Bermeja up with a nuclear bomb."

I chuckled. "Yes, I did hear that one. And I understand that political feathers are unusually ruffled along with extremely high economic tensions."

"Enough said then, Captain. I just wanted to give a fellow sailor a peek at the coming weather."

"That is very appreciated."

Petty Officer Morales pulled a card from his shirt pocket and handed it to me. "My personal mobile number is here. If you run into something more than . . . survey results, you can call anytime."

I took the card, noticing the petty officer's first name. "Thank you, Eduardo."

"You're very welcome, Michael."

Twenty minutes later, lines were retrieved and coiled and *Water Horse* steamed west with the morning sun at our backs, and our bow curling a crystal blue wake, providing a free surf for a pair of playful dolphins. We were on our way. On our way to what seemed a bit murkier than it had a few days ago, but hell, that hadn't stopped us any other time. Harper was on the bow, tongue out, with his gray furry ears waving in the breeze. Nothing but the enjoyment of the sun, the feel of the wind, and the excitement of "the going." I knew exactly how he felt.

Chapter 8

JERRY STYLES STOOD AT THE HELM, steering us north-north-west. Dr. Cruz and I stood at the nav station, examining the chart of the southern Gulf of Mexico. Our guest geologist carefully marked the coordinates of our first mystery island, Bermeja, on the chart as he explained some of the geological features of the region. "Two hundred fifty million years ago, as the supercontinent Pangaea broke apart, the Yucatán Shelf was formed. As sea levels rose and fell, the shallower water remained here, just before the Gulf plunges into the Sigsbee Deep."

The aptly named "Sigsbee Deep" is a part of the Gulf of Mexico where the bottoms drops to an abyss of eleven thousand feet of dark, largely unexplored mystery.

Dr. Cruz continued, "Back from the edge of the shelf, approximately fifty kilometers, is where we find some very small and isolated cays. Researchers believe that Bermeja was one of those small cays, along with the second island in question, Isla Escondida, further to the east."

"Has there ever been anything on any of the cays?" I asked.

"No. They are all too small for any development. Fishing can be good near them, but they are too far from the mainland for the casual sport fisherman, and the serious game angler would rather fish near the edge of the shelf where the bottom falls away. That's where many record billfish are caught."

"Doctor, couldn't a storm simply wash one of these islands away?"

"It's certainly not impossible. But people have documented these cays here for many hundreds of years. The storm history in the Gulf has been largely consistent for the last twenty years, so the probability that two islands would disappear in such a short period seems unlikely. But that's what we're here to find out."

"Understood," I said. "Jas and Morgan are down in the lab working on a few mods to our ROV. Would you like to join me, to see what they are up to?"

Mateo smiled broadly. "Very much, Captain."

We entered the camera shop, and Morgan and Jas were hovering around our bright yellow ROV. We affectionately called the partially autonomous ROV "Woody" because some of its design features were modeled after ROVs from the legendary research group out of the Woods Hole Oceanographic Institution in Massachusetts. Morgan and Jas both stood as we entered the room.

"Did you two set a star to sail by?" Morgan asked.

"We did," I answered. "Jerry is steaming us that way. Tell us what you've got."

Jas took over and she moved around the table to reveal more of the ROV to Dr. Cruz. When she passed in front of me, I caught a pleasant hint of chocolate and spice. *Is that perfume? She never wears perfume. Why is she wearing perfume?*

Jas gave a playful flip of her brunette hair as she launched into her tech walk-through. "We just upgraded the acoustic-modem communication system on Woody, which increases our range and provides zero latency on the video return from the three onboard cameras. But the real mod for this trip is this bottom sample extractor that Morgan engineered. This small stainless straw device here inserts itself into the bottom and collects the sample. As more samples are collected, they get pushed into this coiled tube at precise intervals. The ROV automatically records the precise location of each sample. Back in the lab, we can download the nav data and it automatically matches the samples with the positions where they were extracted.

"That is amazing, Ms. Jas," gushed the geologist.

I looked at Morgan with his wrinkle, now on my forehead.

"That's impressive, Morgan. Nice work," I said.

"It should make the sample collection faster," Morgan said. "Jas also updated the firmware so that as soon as Woody's sample tube is full, he'll return to the surface so a fresh coil of tube can get installed, putting the ROV back on station in under an hour."

"As usual, you two have over-delivered. What's Woody's battery operating time?"

"Six hours, and the team can load a fresh battery during a sample coil change," Jas said.

"Captain, I intend to collect samples as well, along with making notes on any geological observations we may find. Would it be possible for Ms. Jas to assist me on those dives?"

"Jas will be operating the ROV," I said.

Jas looked down at the table.

"Ahh, I was going to operate the ROV this go around because of the new sample mechanism," Morgan said.

"I'd be happy to assist, Captain," Jas said.

"That sounds like a great plan," I said. But Morgan's smart-ass grin didn't slip my detection as he spun, returning a screwdriver to the tool chest.

As I exited the camera shop, Jas caught me out on the side deck. "Hey, Michael, are you really okay with me assisting Dr. Cruz with the dive and sample collection?"

"Absolutely. I'd never hear the end of it if Morgan didn't get to test out his new gadget for the first dive." The part about Morgan and the ROV was true, but I couldn't tell how well I had sold the "absolutely" line. "Dr. Cruz seems to really like you."

"Oh Captain, he's all teeth and tan." She grinned. "But he does go on, doesn't he?"

I screwed on my best crooked smile. "Don't make me change my mind."

Jas stepped up and gently patted me twice on the chest. "Roger that, Captain." And she turned and left.

As I stood there with my face hanging out, an old memory from home cropped up. More learning happened on the front porch of our old house than any classroom I ever sat in. The evening that rushed into my memory was no different. I was sitting on the steps of the front porch, again. I was maybe fifteen years old. The numerous "what's on your mind, son?" questions posed by Mom during dinner, I answered with the typical teen, "nuthing." So there I sat on the front steps, fuming about some teen drama with a girl. Dad came out and sat down in a chair behind me. He stayed quiet for a long time, then said, "There's a universal truth about women that you probably need to learn sooner rather than later. Girls feel stuff different than we do, son, it's just a fact. In the emotions department, a woman works with an entire orchestra. She has all those different instruments, making all different kinds of notes and sounds. Men, on the other hand, tend to work with a much simpler musical combo. In fact, most of men are stuck with one of those tiny toy pianos, just plinking away, trying to play chopsticks with two fingers."

I smiled at the memory, shook my head, tucked my toy piano under my arm, and headed for the bridge.

We continued our northwest trek through another postcard worthy day in the Gulf. At nine p.m., I sat at my desk with a short pour of Powers Irish whiskey. The smell of good whiskey is rich and warm. Admittedly, when abused, it's destroyed countless lives over the centuries. Enjoyed responsibly, with proper respect, the complex aroma of a quality spirit always made me feel a connection to a nameless legacy. For centuries, explorers, captains, generals, and presidents have sat and inhaled the smokey aroma of carefully aged distilling while contemplating decisions and actions that changed the world. I didn't have any lofty notions about

my own contemplations, but I always felt some small connection to the shared tradition of the act.

With my laptop open, I scrolled, catching up on email.
Clicking my way through the mass deletions of junk, I saw
a new message from Ellie. I clicked on her message, expecting the "enjoyed my trip, love you both" thank you
note. But instead, it was nearly ten pages of research on the
Mexico Bermeja saga. Our sister's investigative brain had
already been busy. After scanning through just a few pages,
it was clear to me that high political tensions and wild ac-
cusations surrounding Bermeja were a gross understate-
ment. The most disturbing bit was the theory put forward
by one official accusing members within the Mexican government of actively taking bribes to look the other way
while American big oil destroyed the islands, taking more
oil exploration territory for themselves. This expedition
was far more complicated than it appeared on the surface. I
wasn't so much surprised as amused. Government officials
not divulging the whole story and fighting among themselves? Shocker.

Then there was our guest, Dr. Cruz. He seemed to have
enough influence to tilt this in a few different directions.
We're not geologists, if he wanted to manipulate the data and
suggest evidence that foul play was involved, would we be
able to dispute it? If he dismissed everything as natural oc-

currences, he'd be able to clear anyone involved in covering up attempts to artificially remove the islands.

I could still hear him gush over Jas's work on the ROV. *That is amazing, Ms. Jas.* I snickered as I drained my last sip, enjoying the warmth all the way down.

A portable radio sitting on my desk came to life. It was Beau Benson on helm duty. I was to relieve him in a half hour. "Captain . . . helm, over."

I picked up the radio. "Go, helm."

"Captain, we're coming up on some debris about a half mile out, ten degrees off the starboard bow, would you like to take a look?"

"On my way, Beau."

Inside the pilothouse, Beau had positioned the remote spotlight to shine on the pieces of debris as we closed on its position. Morgan stepped into the cabin seconds behind me, he had heard the call on the radio. As the patch got closer, we could see it was flotsam from a vessel. A few seat cushions, bits of wood, and other unidentified broken parts. I stepped out on the pilothouse side deck to get a closer look as Beau slowed and eased alongside the floating patch of disregard that I was afraid was a sign of something uglier.

"What do you think happened here, Captain?" Beau asked.

"Looks like an explosion. I don't think a collision would have created this much debris." I answered.

"Some of the dive boats down here are pretty rough from a maintenance standpoint," Morgan said.

"It'd take a lot of fuel and perfect conditions to blow a boat into this many pieces," Beau replied.

I spotted something in the drifting collection that made me rush down the stairs to the main deck and pull a boat hook off the bulkhead. Leaning against the rail, I lowered the hook end of the pole down to the water and snagged the object that had caught my eye. Once on deck, I turned the life-saving ring over to reveal partially burned letters stenciled around the perimeter of the ring. The letter L had been spared by the flames along with the word EXPLORER. Morgan stepped beside me and dropped a marker buoy into the water in the center of the debris field. It was bright yellow and had a GPS tracker attached to the long rod, topped with a reflective signal flag. I keyed the mic on my radio. "Beau, mark this position on the plotter."

"Roger that, Cap."

"From the missing dive boat?" Morgan asked.

"Sure seems that way. With L-EXPLORER, I'd tell Pat and Vanna I wanted to solve the puzzle."

Morgan pointed to another object in the debris patch and said, "What's that?"

It was black and harder to see in the water. I lowered the hook into the water and turned the item over with the tip of the hook. It was a neoprene divers boot, with a foot still zipped into place. I hooked the loop in the strap on the back of the bootie and lifted it up and carefully placed it upright on the deck. Three inches of skin and bone protruded from the top of the black neoprene. My stomach roiled. The victim count in the Gulf was rising and those quiet voices in my head were getting much louder. That wound deep in my chest cracked open a little more. There was more going on here, and it kept getting uglier.

"Well, that complicates things," I said.

"Yep," said Morgan. "Don't touch it. I'll bag it and get it on ice. Let's have Jas take some pictures."

I pulled the radio off my belt. "Beau, we found a foot. Buzz Jas's cabin and have her grab a camera to take some photos."

There was a slight pause. "Roger that, Cap," Beau answered, the somberness clear in his voice, sensing that whatever we were retrieving from the debris field couldn't be good.

Back in the pilothouse, I checked my watch, quarter to ten. We were nine hours from our first set of search coordinates. Dr. Cruz was now standing silently near the helm, taking in all the activity. "Does this have anything to do with what the petty officer spoke to you about before we departed?" he asked.

I looked Mateo in the eyes for a beat and then answered, "Yes, it does. The petty officer asked us to be on the lookout for a dive boat that was overdue in port, with six passengers aboard. Beau, after Jas takes some shots, let's make two slow circles in the area, increasing our distance from the debris each time. I want to make sure there's no one else floating out here, waiting for rescue."

"You got it."

Beau began our circles at idle speed and slowly swept the wide beam of the searchlight methodically across the calm water's surface. Morgan used binoculars to aid in the search. I reached into my shirt pocket and retrieved Petty Officer Morales card and dialed his number.

"Morales," he answered after two rings.

"Eduardo, this is Michael Gannon aboard *Water Horse*, sorry for the late call. I think we just came across debris from your missing dive boat, *Coral Explorer*. We found a partially burned life ring along with some cushions and wood bulkhead pieces. And . . . we found a foot in a dive bootie." I let that absorb for a second and added, "We're making some circles to see if anyone's in the water."

I could hear him riffling on a desk looking for pen and

paper, and with a resigned sigh, the petty officer said, "What's your position?"

I stepped over to the plotter to read the saved latitude and longitude. "22°08′59″ north, by 89°44′08″ west."

The petty officer read the coordinates back, and I confirmed. "We've marked the debris with a signal buoy. I'll message you the tracking data. I kept the life ring aboard and we've bagged the foot and put it on ice."

"Understood, Captain. Thank you for stopping and investigating. I'll dispatch a boat right away."

Completely convinced of what he would say, I reluctantly asked, "Do you want us to stay on station until you arrive?"

"No, Captain. If you make your circles and find nothing else, proceed to your destination. I'll leave at first light on another boat and meet you, if you'll send me the position of your intended location. I can have a team at the debris field in four hours on a fast patrol vessel. Thank you for dropping the marker, that will be helpful."

Relieved and surprised, I said, "Understood." I read the petty officer our destination coordinates and added, "We'll proceed west-northwest and should be on station just before dawn. Reach out on the radio when you get close."

There was a short pause on the line. "Keep a weather eye, Captain."

"Roger that, Eduardo." And I ended the call, as I watched

Beau make another sweep with the searchlight. I motioned for Morgan to step out on the wing deck with me, out of earshot of Dr. Cruz. As Morgan stepped out, he closed the pilothouse door behind him before asking, "Things are adding up that color outside the lines of coincidence, don't you think?"

"What would it take to blow a thirty-six-foot dive boat into this many pieces?"

"An engine room filled with gas vapors will certainly explode, but this looks more like C-4 to me," he said.

"Why blow up a dive boat?" I asked.

"Didn't the petty officer say that sometimes tourists come across narcos doing deals out here? Maybe this boat approached something worse."

"It sure looks that way. El just sent me an email with some detailed research on the Bermeja hunt, and there's many more moving parts and angry players than Ms. Vega disclosed."

Morgan gave me a mocked look of surprise.

"Yeah, yeah, I know—shocker."

Chapter 9

At half past seven a.m., the chart plotter began chiming our arrival at the last known location of Bermeja. On the trip here, Dr. Cruz tweaked the firmware of our onboard sonar system to detect more subtle density changes in the bottom as we searched. Two minutes before we arrived at the provided coordinates, the color-coded density readings on the sonar had indeed shown differences from the surrounding bottom, even though we detected no change in the water's depth. I stood at the helm looking in every direction but saw no sign of anything but water. If a small sandy island had ever peeked above the surface of the Gulf, it was now gone. The sea conditions were calm, with scattered puffy clouds and temps in the upper seventies. Beau stood on the bow and I signaled him to lower our anchor in sixty-five feet of water.

The plan for the first day of our survey mission was simple. Dr. Cruz and Jas would take bottom samples and make notes of any visual anomalies in the bottom along this area where the sonar indicated differences in seafloor density. I would record ultra-high-definition video and stills of the area and keep an eye on the ROV as the new sampling mechanism systematically searched a grid across the first search area. Morgan would monitor the ROV from the control center on the surface and Beau would off-load filled sample tubes, reload new sample coils, and refresh ROV batteries. Rudy would—

"Woof!"

Harper came bounding into the pilothouse. The change in his appearance in just a few days was nothing short of miraculous. His unruly gray coat shined and his eyes were bright. Rudy stepped in immediately behind him and said, "Harper, it's the captain."

Harper quickly sat and raised his right paw up to his right floppy ear.

"At ease, sailor," I said.

Harper lowered his paw and approached me for an ear scratch.

"Morning, Cap, I'm going to be doing the final wiring on

the new underwater lighting system we mounted on the hull, unless you need me for something else."

"No, that sounds good. I look forward to seeing them in action."

"Gonna look like someone flipped the switch to the sun under the boat." He smiled.

"Well, okay then," I said.

I felt a low growl before I heard it, and Rudy and I looked out on the bridge deck where Harper stood locked in on something approaching from the west. Rudy raised an eyebrow, and we both stepped outside on to the pilothouse wing deck to see what had Harper's attention. Rudy and I scanned the horizon, but I couldn't see or hear anything. But Harper remained locked on to the western horizon with his deep bubbling, almost constant growl.

"What ya see, sailor?" Rudy asked.

"There," I said, as I pointed at a black spec low in the sky.

The tiny object grew, and it appeared to be on a heading directly at our position. Seconds later, we could hear the distinctive thumping of a helicopter as it approached.

"We expecting company?" Rudy asked.

"Not by chopper. We're expecting Petty Officer Morales to come out by boat to retrieve the foot. But that's the wrong direction for him."

As the chopper got closer, it appeared to be a corporate civilian bird. A sleek, black jet-copter less than three hundred feet off the surface of the water, as it continued to head straight for our position. The whine of the turbine grew almost deafening as it closed in on us without altering its heading one degree. I pulled out my phone and held the camera shutter button down, snapping a string of stills as the black bird buzzed our position at over two hundred knots, rattling every port on the boat. As soon as it passed, the radio erupted with chatter from every crew member. Morgan's voice broke through the noise. "What the hell was that!"

"We just got buzzed by a corporate jet-copter," I answered.

"The Gulf is a big place. Think that was necessary?" Rudy said.

"They'll probably laugh about it all afternoon at the club," I said.

"More jack-wagons. I'll be in the electrical locker. Come on, Harper."

"Grrrr."

We'd no sooner shook off the low pass of the chopper when I saw a boat approaching from the southeast. There seemed to be a lot of activity for being anchored hundreds of miles from shore in the middle of the Gulf of Mexico. I raised the binoculars and could see it was a military patrol boat. It would be Petty Officer Morales, coming to retrieve the grizzly recovered evidence. I picked up a radio. "Beau and Jerry, will you make preparations to take a patrol boat alongside?"

"Will do, Captain," Beau answered.

I met the petty officer on the aft deck as he stepped up from our boarding platform.

"Wow, Petty Officer Morales, you're becoming a daily guest. Do I need to assign you a bunk?"

Morales chuckled. "It does seem as if we are visiting on a regular basis, Captain."

"Coming for a pickup, I imagine."

"Unfortunately, yes."

I gave the petty officer a full brief of our discovery and described the scene as clearly as I could remember. Morgan met us out on the aft deck with a small Styrofoam cooler with something taped to the top of the lid and the partially burned life ring from the *Coral Explorer*.

"Petty Officer Morales, this is my brother and my partner, Morgan Gannon."

The petty officer extended his hand. "Very nice to meet you, Morgan."

"You as well, Petty Officer. Thanks for making the run all the way out here. You're the second visitor of the morning already."

Morales looked confused. "Second visitor?"

"We had a corporate jet-copter buzz us shortly before you arrived," I said.

Morales rolled his eyes. "We do have our share of citizens from the peninsula with bigger bank accounts than brains, I'm afraid."

"We put some cold packs in here and the thumb drive taped to the top has photos we took of the debris field."

Morales lifted the lid to the cooler and peeked inside, frowned, and shook his head. "That will be very helpful. Thank you both for your assistance. Any guesses on what happened out there?"

"An explosion, for sure," I said. "But whether they ran afoul of someone or a tired dive captain forgot to run the engine room blower before cranking a gas engine, will take further investigation of the debris."

"My team finished recovery of all they could find this morning. I'll get your marker buoy back to you next time you're in port."

"No worries," Morgan said.

"Gentlemen, I sincerely hope the rest of your survey mission proceeds less eventful than the last few days."

"Us too." I laughed.

"I'm going to get this back to the lab. Michael, you have my number."

"I do, Eduardo. Thanks."

I watched as the petty officer cast off and throttled the patrol boat up on plane, creating a foaming white stern wake that disappeared off to the southeast. Morgan stepped beside me as I watched what I hoped was our last visitor for a while.

"Less eventful? He doesn't know us at all, does he?" Morgan said.

"I'm afraid not."

Our three person dive party splashed off the aft dive platform into water clarity that was spectacular, with a hundred-plus feet of visibility. The sun cast shimmering beams down toward the sandy bottom. The columns of light reflected off small sediment and tiny fish as it stretched into the depths, creating shiny diamond-like sparkles in the gin clear water. Gulf temperatures were a balmy seventy-three degrees, making our lightweight neoprene wet suits perfect. My video camera rig contained two cameras. The custom underwater housing held both an 8K video camera and a twenty-four mega-pixel still camera. Morgan and Jas designed and built the custom housing for me, and it was a joy to operate. They'd tailored all the controls and functions to my exact preferences.

Dr. Cruz and Jas took the lead, descending away from the surface as I held back to capture an establishing shot of the area. The filtered sunlight and the clear water that transitioned to aqua blue in the distance made an incredible shot of the two divers slowly kicking their fins into the distance. The high-pitched whirr of Woody's maneuvering motors caught my attention as they spun into action and I looked up to the surface in time to see the bright yellow body make for the bottom, beginning its programmed sampling mission.

Our full-face masks and regulators contained a voice activated com system, allowing us to stay in communication under the water and with Morgan on the surface. I spoke, activating the mic. "Coms check. Morgan, you have us topside?"

"Loud and clear," he answered.

"Jas, Mateo, how do you read?" I called.

"Good for Jas."

"I read you loud and clear, Captain," answered the doctor.

"Let's do a check in every five minutes, roger?"

"Roger that," Jas called.

As I reached the bottom, the remarks and observations from the government surveys of the area were consistent with what I could now see for myself. Nothing seemed unusual about the bottom. White contoured sand shaped by waves and currents stretched in all directions. Dr. Cruz and Jas began taking bottom samples seventy feet to my right.

Woody reached the bottom and went straight to work with its stainless tube inserting itself into the bottom at regular intervals. I captured several close-up shots of the ROV and the newly designed sample collector articulating in and out of the sand. It surprised me that I was able to even snap fine detail shots of each sample being pushed bit by bit into the translucent sample tubing coil as it rested in its position on the top of the machine.

Thirty minutes later, the three of us scanned across the far western edge of the search area, and I noticed something different on the bottom, out on the edge of my visibility. I gave a couple of lazy kicks and propelled myself toward the anomaly. The bottom sand in this area had fallen into a crevice. As I got closer, I could see it was a limestone fissure about two feet wide. I spoke into the coms. "Mateo, Jas, come see what you make of this."

I captured some footage and a few stills of the depression as Jas and Mateo glided up to the far side of the crevice. "Mateo, are there limestone caverns under the seafloor in the Gulf?" I asked.

"Yes, in many places, there are large limestone formations and salt domes," he said as he swam closer and began investigating deeper into the crevice. The doctor scooped handfuls of sand from the gap in the limestone. I set my camera down on the flat bottom to one side of the ditch and, with no words between us, Jas and I started scooping handfuls of sand along with Mateo. Within a few minutes, we had pulled enough sand out of the depression that the ditch was now two feet deep. The walls of the limestone seem to widen the deeper we dug. As I scooped into the sand, my fingertips struck something hard. I sifted the handful and came up with a metal ring about six inches in diameter and one inch wide. It was rusty but didn't look ancient. Neither Jas nor Dr. Cruz noticed the object, and I slipped it into my waist bag and continued to scoop.

The tool that Dr. Cruz used to take his bottom samples was a metal tube one inch in diameter and about three feet long. He inserted it vertically into the bottom and a half twist of the wrist would capture a three-inch-long sample of sand in the bottom of the tube. Then you could release the sample into a series of bags that were sealed and held in a larger collection bag that Jas carried.

Dr. Cruz took the sample tube and pushed it into the bottom of the hole we'd created, and I could tell he encountered very little resistance as the tube penetrated all the way up to the handle. He pulled it out and plunged it back into the bottom of the hole. Three stabs later, sand started slowly spilling down into a hollow opening in the limestone. The void widened quickly, and I felt my buoyancy change, causing me to extend a finned foot against the upper edge of the crevice. "Back away!" was all I could get out before a massive section of sandy bottom plunged into the cavern below.

Chapter 10

JAS LOCKED EYES WITH ME as the powerful downward current created by the cave-in overpowered her, and for the first time since we'd met, her eyes held an intensity I'd not ever seen. She clawed at the water with her cupped hands and her powerful legs kicked her fins to prevent being sucked into the cavern below, but she was losing the battle. My arms and legs tingled as the adrenaline surged, and I shot into the sinkhole. I wedged my back on one side of the crevice and jammed an extended leg on the opposite side. I thrust my hand as far as I could reach through the blinding cloud of bubbles and sediment and found Jas's gloved hand, grasping it, just before she slipped completely out of reach. Sand, silt, and bubbles swirled in a blinding cloud around us as I wrestled her from the hole. In my frantic pulling to free her, the regulator valve on her dive tank banged against the side of the crevice wall and pulled away from the valve. Now an even larger torrent of bubbles poured from her tank, further obscuring our already nonexistent visibility, adding to the chaos of the situation. As quickly as it started, the sand spilling into the sinkhole slowed and the pull of the current eased. I continued to hold tight to Jas. With her free hand, she pulled the quick release buckles on her tank and let it fall into the darkness. Her full-face mask was now flooding, so she peeled it off, dropped it, and calmly reached for my back up regulator, inserting it into her mouth. Seconds later, she gave me the okay sign and didn't seem to be in any distress. My heart still pounded in my chest, but I worked to slow my breathing as I assessed our situation.

The water clarity returned slowly, and I spoke into our coms. "Dr. Cruz, you okay?"

The sand settled and I could see Mateo just outside the crevice, staring into the blackness of the sinkhole. "Mateo! Are you okay?"

My second call shook him out of his daze. "Sí. Sorry, Captain. I knew caverns existed under the seafloor, I've just never seen one before."

"Let's get topside, but we need to make one safety stop on the way. We're going to take it nice and slow."

With his game face back in place, Mateo flashed the okay sign as we prepared to surface. I guided Jas off to the side of the crevice and picked up the camera rig, snapping it to my utility belt behind my waist. Together, we slowly started our ascent with plans to stop at thirty feet for a safety stop. I spoke to engage the coms. "Morgan, we're headed up. Can you and Beau meet us on the platform, please?"

"On our way, brother."

Checking my depth reading, we stopped thirty feet below the surface and surveyed our surroundings. I made eye contact with Jas and she gave me the okay signal. "Mateo, you good?"

"Good to go, Captain."

We paused another ten seconds and then we slowly continued our accent. We broke the surface at the boarding platform and Beau extended a hand, helping Jas out first, followed by Dr. Cruz, then me. There were two portable benches we placed on the aft deck when we were conducting any dive operations and Jas sat down on the end of one. I quickly stripped off my mask and tank and knelt in front of her, and put my hand on her shoulder. "You really, okay?"

"Michael, I'm fine. You caught me, thank you," she said, smiling, looking very directly into my eyes.

I could have lost her. She was an arm's length away and I could have lost her, I thought.

I held my gaze a beat longer than I usually allowed my-self, then stood.

"Mateo, are you good?"

"Yes, Captain, I'm okay. Just still amazed."

"What happened down there?" Morgan asked.

"We discovered a massive limestone cavern under the sand bottom. I was probing into the crevice with a sample rod and, in an instant, it opened up into a sinkhole that threatened to swallow up Ms. Jas," Mateo said.

Wiping the dripping water off her face, Jas said, "Morgan, I lost my rig. Sorry about that."

"Gear is cheap. You are not. Got that?"

Jas smiled and nodded.

"Beau and I are going to retrieve Woody and we'll get the samples to the lab. Why don't we wrap dive operations for the day and regroup this afternoon," Morgan said.

The afternoon passed quietly. Morgan and Jas worked with Dr. Cruz to collect the bottom samples from the ROV collec-tion coils and download the position data for each sample. I got cleaned up, and as I left my cabin, I stopped and picked up the metal ring that I had set on my desk and hit the galley for a snack. In the fridge, I found a large Tupperware of Rudy's chili and heated up a cup. The chili was warming as I ate quietly at the galley table when Morgan stepped in. "Hey, we'll have some sample data ready to review shortly. Come down to the lab when you're done."

"I will. Hey, got any clue what this might be?" I tossed the metal ring to him. He caught it and looked at it for several seconds.

"Doesn't look that old," he said. "But I don't have a clue what it is. You find that on the bottom here?"

"Yep."

"I'd check with Rudy. He's probably seen or handled about every kind of marine hardware ever built."

"I'm headed there next. Then I'll head to the lab."

"You okay?" Morgan asked.

"I'm fine. Just got out of hand down there quick."

"Everyone's okay. We'll take a beat and start again. We've got time."

I nodded and shoveled in another spoonful. Morgan tossed the metal ring back to me before he turned to leave and I caught it, setting the rusty object on the table and covering it with my napkin, before finishing my chili. As I washed my bowl, I thought about Morgan's statement about time, and wasn't sure that he was right this time. People were getting hurt and now a close call with my own crew. My gut was telling me the clock was ticking. Counting down to what, I didn't know. But so far, it was nothing good. I rinsed and dried, then went to consult our resident old salt.

I found our engineer sitting on a stool at his workbench, making notes in his maintenance log. When I stepped into the compartment, Harper sat up and panted expectantly, tail pinging out a cheerful alarm against the metal legs of the stool.

Rudy turned to see who had entered. "Hey, Cap. You had a little scare down there, I understand."

"A little," I said. "Spooked me. Jas, on the other hand, was cool as a cucumber."

Rudy snickered. "She's a tough gal, for sure. You know she missed a new world record by only two meters on her last competitive dive."

"I didn't know that," I said.

"A big part of free diving is convincing your body you aren't going to die, when every ounce of you is screaming to breathe. She had to become a master at staying cool and slowing everything down."

"I saw that today. Did she ever say why she left the sport?"

"She doesn't talk about it much, but I think she got involved with her coach and that ended badly."

"Hmm." That's all I had, just . . . hmm. The door on all that would have to close for now. Things were moving fast and my head needed to be in one place only, and it wasn't thinking about Jas and diving coaches.

I took the metal ring I found on our dive and placed it on Rudy's bench in front of him. I gave Harper a scratch behind the ear and he leaned his big furry head against my leg to soak up the gesture. "What do you make of that?" I asked, pointing to the rusty find.

Rudy picked up the ring and turned it in his hand a few times. "Looks like a locking ring from a section of flexible hose. I've seen similar locking rings on dredging hoses."

"A dredging hose? Are you sure?"

"You kidding me? I spent a year-one-month wrenching on a dredge rig during a hot July when the economy got slow. Never been so glad to get off a boat in my life. Where'd you find this?"

"On the bottom, in the limestone crevice, that almost swallowed us."

Rudy raised his eyebrows. "Really? Well, that seems an unlikely spot to find something like this. What did Dr. Cruz say?"

"I haven't mentioned it just yet."

"You don't trust him yet, do you?"

"After reading more about this whole thing, I don't trust anyone just yet."

Rudy held the metal ring up and rotated it a few times. "Nothing wrong with holding your cards close, Captain."

"We'll see if there's anything unusual in the bottom samples, then I'll decide if I want to mention what I found to our marine geologist."

"Not sure it means anything, but Harper here seems to sniff test the doctor okay. He allowed him a belly scratch this morning."

"I'll take any barometer I can get right now."

Pointing to the metal ring, I said, "I'm going to leave that with you for now."

"It'll be in my top drawer here whenever you want it."

Down in the lab, Jas and Morgan were arranging small sample bottles, each three inches long, into trays that held the individual bottles in two dozen separate divided spaces. Dr. Cruz was working at the computer station, and seconds after I entered, the printer started whirring, printing out data. He picked up the printed sheets and brought them over to the larger worktable.

"Captain! You're just in time."

"Anything noteworthy?" I asked.

"Yes, actually," he said, spreading the papers out as we all surrounded the table. One sheet had a printed map of the search area with red-colored dots and corresponding numbers marking each location where he and the ROV collected the samples. The second sheet was a spreadsheet listing each sample number, followed by the top five chemical compounds found in each sample.

"You can see these samples that were out on the edge of the search area contained all the compounds you would expect. Silica, Calcium carbonate, Feldspar, all common elements found in the sand covering the Gulf bottom. These samples taken more in the center of the target zone contain something that I didn't expect at all."

I leaned over and looked closer at the document. "Lithium?"

Mateo smiled broadly. "Lithium, yes."

"Lithium . . . like the gold rush of the next century, key material in all electric vehicle batteries . . . lithium?" Morgan asked.

"That's the stuff," I answered.

Mateo continued, "It's possible that some of the limestone caverns collect saltwater brines and, over the centuries, it concentrated the lithium. There have been samples taken in salt domes in other parts of the Gulf, but in those cases, there were no considerable traces of the compound found. Perhaps there is something different about this zone of the Gulf."

I put some edge on my next question, and Mateo sensed it. "Doctor, has there been any speculation about lithium being found in this part of the Gulf?"

"No, Captain, nothing. Do you think lithium has anything to do with all this?"

"I don't know, but it's a very interesting part of the puzzle. Is there any sign of radiation in any of the samples?"

"Other than naturally occurring residual radiation, none at all."

"So the American CIA nuking the islands is probably off the table."

"Yes, that seems highly unlikely. Captain, I know Secretary Vega asked you to report in immediately with any significant findings, but could I respectfully ask that we wait until we investigate this a little further?"

And so it begins. "I was already thinking the same thing," I said.

Mateo looked relieved. "I'd like to explore the sinkhole here, then proceed to the recorded location of Isla Escondida."

"Jas, will you make sure that Woody is ready for another dive first thing in the morning?"

"Absolutely, Captain."

"Mateo, will you meet Morgan and I in the pilothouse in ten minutes?"

His face fell slack and any trace of the charisma fell away. " . . . certainly, Captain."

On the way to the pilothouse, I stopped and picked up the rusty metal ring from Rudy's shop, and when I arrived on the bridge, Morgan was pulling the starboard wing door closed and I closed the port side door leaving the three of us standing in the closed space. The geologist seemed somber and intimidated, and that's exactly how I wanted him to feel.

"Dr. Cruz, after some thorough background research from our award-winning investigative reporter sister, the same reporter that uncovered the corporate ties to the missing king crab in the Bering Sea, it seems apparent that there's more to the Bermeja and Isla Escondida matter than is being disclosed. Now, with the discovery of lithium on this site, we're going to need you to put a few cards on the table. To be very blunt, I don't know how to proceed, because I don't think I trust you."

Mateo swallowed hard. "Captain, I don't know if I can trust you."

"Then let's go back to Marinero Salado. I'll buy the cervezas this time and we'll call 'no harm, no foul.' But I'm not going to put my crew and ship in any situation with this much fog. I'm sure you can find another survey team."

Mateo looked at his feet for a long moment, then met my stare. "Captain, I am a geologist, but I am also working for Mexican National Security, CISEN. My involvement with CISEN has been kept highly classified and my background within the government has been tightly constrained to my work as a scientist. There have been suspicions that Minister Vega and a small syndicate within the government have been taking bribes from global oil interests to alter our country's oil exploration future. Minister Vega has postured herself by aggressively investigating the matter, and if she cannot use my data to sell the misidentification or natural erosion angle, she will push to blame the US government and your CIA. But CISEN now has intel that other unknown players outside our government are involved. The challenge has been gathering any meaningful proof. When Minister Vega's office reached out to you, CISEN and I researched your background and saw it as the perfect opportunity to uncover the evidence we needed to expose them."

"Why didn't CISEN approach us directly?" Morgan asked.

"Because too much information has been leaking back to the syndicate, so we kept it within a small group of intelligence officials and myself, and we report directly to the President of Mexico. My scientific credentials made me the obvious choice for Vega to appear that she was conducting a legitimate investigation. As you could see from our first observations, the site of Bermeja seems perfectly natural. The traces of lithium would have been interesting, but the data may still point to a natural explanation."

"Dr. Cruz, the safety of my crew and my boat means more to me than most captains, because this is my family and my home. My first inclination would be to drop you in a life raft, call the Mexican Navy on your behalf, and run north at flank speed."

"Captain, I assure you, we did not anticipate running into trouble on the survey part of this mission. We just knew the pieces were not adding up and Secretary Vega's motives seemed suspect."

"What happens if Morgan and I walk away right now?"

"Then, as you say, 'no harm no foul.' But if you help us expose Minister Vega and her associates, the Mexican government is prepared to offer a significant bonus to your compensation."

"I'm much more interested that no more innocent people get hurt, because I think that the shot up skiff and destroyed dive boat are all a part of this."

"Preventing anyone else from being hurt is our sincere desire as well. When we found out that Secretary Vega had contacted you, again, things seemed to align well with our goals."

"Can you be a little more specific?" I asked.

"Your brother's former experience," Mateo said.

"So, you're aware of Morgan's unique background?"

"We are indeed, and I have instructions to provide any further resources and assistance needed and to grant you the highest government approval for your operational preferences."

"Dr. Cruz, I know you are working for CISEN, but have you had any other training besides geology?" Morgan asked.

"I spent six years with GAFE special forces. I went back to university to finish my degree in geology eight years ago. And my background with GAFE has been completely sanitized from all government records."

Morgan raised an eyebrow as he caught my eye and gave me a subtle nod.

"GAFE is no joke, Dr. Cruz," Morgan remarked.

"That part of your brain never switches off, but after some time, many of us seek more . . . positive pursuits."

Morgan nodded with understanding, extending his hand, and the two men shook like only warriors could, no matter what army or battlefield they may have stood on.

I stepped over and handed Mateo the metal ring, and he held it up, inspecting it. "My engineer says that's a locking ring to dredging hose."

Mateo's eyes grew wide. "A dredge?"

"Dr. Cruz, can you and I agree it's time we dispense with any further secrets?"

"Yes, Captain, we can."

"We'll continue for now, but will you excuse Morgan and I to discuss this further?"

"Certainly, Captain."

When Mateo left the pilothouse, I looked at Morgan. "What do you think?"

"I agree with you. All this does seem to be related. How it's related, I don't know, but definitely related."

"What do you want to do?" I asked.

"This is a largely a business decision, so I'll leave that to you. You know that I'll back the call no matter what. I do like the phrase 'approval for your operational preferences.'"

"Yeah, I thought you might like that one. I just don't want to put the crew in danger."

"I think you may be underestimating their resolve," Morgan said.

"I might be, but it's my job to protect them," I said.

"You always do, brother. Try and get some rest. I'll be in my shop."

Pulling out my phone, I flipped through the pictures I'd taken of the chopper as it thundered a hundred feet over our superstructure. Most of the images were too blurry to make anything out, but one was clear enough for me to zoom in on the back section of the passenger cabin. In silver stylized letters, I could read the words Goddard Petroleum. I hit the home button on my phone and tapped a number in my favorites. The phone rang twice.

"I've been freezing my butt off for less than a week and

you've already found something, haven't you? I knew it! I knew I should have stayed."

"Hi, El, how are you?"

"Save it, Mike-Mike, what do you have?"

"Maybe nothing. Will you see what you can dig up on Goddard Petroleum?"

I could hear the subtle clack of keys as she typed.

"Goddard Petroleum, out of Austin, Texas. CEO is Steven Goddard. The company's only ten years old, so a relatively new player in that business. I'll dig further and get back to you. I'll bet that muscled, big smile guy is all walking around tanned and shirtless. And here I am kicking slush off my shoes and putting extra blankets on the bed."

I let her finish the rant before asking, "Could you see if there's been any talk of lithium exploration in the Gulf?"

"Lithium? Like lithium for batteries—lithium?"

"Yeah, we found traces of lithium where Bermeja should be."

"Okay . . . Story's getting juicier now."

I gave her the rundown on what we'd discovered on the dive, along with our "cards on the table" discussion with Dr. Cruz.

"El, from everything you sent me earlier and with what Cruz has divulged, we need to keep this very under wraps, yeah."

"If I were there, I'd punch you right in the stomach, Michael Gannon. Who do you think I am?"

"Okay, okay, easy, Rambo. I just needed to say the words."

"Well, say those words to someone you don't know if you can trust. I'm your sister."

"Yes, you are. I'm sorry."

"How's my brother?"

"He's fine. We ran into an old buddy of his from the Teams in a dive bar in Cancun. Biggest guy I've ever seen. Almost got in a bar fight."

"See! That's what I'm talking about. Mrs. Vincent, two doors down, knocked on my door at eleven last night to say she'd lost her cat, and you're watching giants in bar fights."

"Come back down after this assignment. We'll make it up to you. New Year's Eve in the Keys, okay?"

"I'm packing already. But seriously, you two be careful, yeah."

"Always. Call me when you know more. . . . Hey, El?"

"Yeah?"

"What's the cat's name?"

CLICK

Chapter 11

THE NEXT MORNING, the doctor and I had a quiet talk on the bow about disclosure ground rules going forward and we came to an acceptable understanding for now. So by nine a.m., Mateo, Jas, and I hovered on either side of the sinkhole we discovered at a depth of seventy-two feet, watching closely as Woody the ROV maneuvered down and disappeared into the limestone. As the small remote craft slipped into the darkness, its light array automatically switched on, giving us our first glimpse inside the cavern. No one would enter until Morgan had conducted a thorough look via Woody's onboard camera systems. So we all crowded around the opening, trying to grab a glimpse inside the mysterious grotto.

Morgan relayed what he was seeing on the camera feed through our coms, as he watched high and dry topside in the edit bay. "The cavern appears to deepen further inside. It must be a massive cave, but it appears to be almost completely filled with sand now. I can see some small recesses up against the ceiling of the cavern, but the passages are too small for me to pilot Woody safely. I think it would be okay to come just inside the opening and take a few samples, but you shouldn't go in much further. The sand looks loose and it could continue to shift around. We have no idea what's below the current floor level."

"Roger that," I said.

Morgan expertly guided the ROV back toward the entrance of the cavern, but it remained inside, providing him a view of the team via the camera as we entered to gather samples. I tied a safety line to Mateo's utility belt and handed Jas the larger coil of line after I paid out enough slack for Mateo to ease into the opening. I would remain in the middle, keeping a watchful eye on his progress.

"Are you ready?" I asked.

Mateo gave me the thumbs up, and he cautiously slipped through the entrance. The lights from the ROV allowed us to watch his progress from our position. We carefully fed him safety line as Mateo descended ten feet to the bottom and then twenty-five feet further north of the opening. He knelt on the bottom and began collecting samples with his tubular probe. As Mateo pushed his sample collector into the soft sand, Morgan slowly panned the lights and cameras of the ROV across the enclosed space. Collecting his last sample, Mateo spoke into his coms. "Okay, that should be enough. I'm coming back out."

Morgan tilted the ROV down to better light the way for Mateo's exit when he said, "Wait. Mateo, what's that? Eight feet to your left, where the limestone wall meets the sand floor."

Mateo turned and, with a gentle kick, maneuvered to the edge of the cavern wall and knelt against the bottom. He fanned his hands across the sand, waving away loose sand, looking for what Morgan may have seen. He stopped suddenly, and let the water's clarity return.

"It's a piece of angled steel," he said. "It runs further into the cavern, but it is buried too deep, and I am unable to move it."

"Good enough, Mateo. Fan off as much sand as you can and we'll let Morgan capture footage and stills of it before we head topside," I said.

"Understood," replied Mateo, as he went to work fanning the loose sand away to reveal an eight-foot section of steel rail about three inches wide on two sides.

Mateo backed away as the visibility improved and Morgan maneuvered the ROV closer to record video and still images of our find. Mateo emerged from the cavern as we coiled the safety line in front of him. Moments later, Morgan piloted Woody back out of the hole and the ROV started rising toward the surface. We followed slowly, stopping again at thirty feet for our safety check.

"Mateo, could you get a sense of how much larger the cavern was before it filled with sand?" Jas asked.

"It looked massive. I could see different branches leading off in many directions. They were just all filled with sand. Captain, what do you make of the steel rail?"

"I don't know yet, but someone had to put it there." I had an inkling of a crazy idea, but it seemed so unlikely, I want to chew on it a while longer. But if this cavern stretched under the footprint of the entire island, maybe it wasn't so crazy.

"I have another piece of equipment on board we should use to take some measurements before we move on," Mateo said.

"You're the scientist," I said. "Just tell us what you need."

"We'll need the ROV," Mateo said.

I nodded, and we resumed our ascent. On the surface, Beau again helped the team from the water and we sat on the benches removing our gear. Morgan knelt nearby, removing the backup memory cards containing photos and video from the ROV cameras. All the image data wirelessly streamed to the central recording servers on board, but the backup cards were always great insurance.

"Morgan, Dr. Cruz has another piece of gear he wants to deploy for some readings. Can you and Jas help adapt Woody to deploy it?"

"You bet. What ya got, Doc?"

"I have a prototype acoustic imaging system. It operates on the same principles as ground penetrating radar, but uses sound waves instead. We can use it to see just how extensive the limestone caverns are in this location."

"New toys? I'm in," said Jas.

Within minutes, our two . . . now three tech geeks knelt around our ROV with pelican cases, tools, and cables spread all around the area of the aft deck. The acoustic imaging module looked similar to a sonar probe, tapered on each end, much like an oversized football. It would hang below the bottom of the ROV on two small steel-strand cables about ten inches long. The data cable exited the football shape on one of the pointed ends and led up to Woody's back where it connected to a data transmitter that would beam the acoustic image data to the ROV control station that was rolled into the ship's editing bay, utilizing our OLED monitor wall.

As a videographer, the edit bay on *Water Horse* was not

only a technological media playground, it was one of the pride and joy spaces for the entire team. Clients aboard always oohed and ahhed whenever they entered the plush compartment. Its comfortable leather easy chairs, subdued lighting, and the memorabilia that covered the walls could have been curated by Jacques Cousteau and Indiana Jones's love child. Then when the monitors covering an entire wall came to life with the ultra-high-definition images from one of our expeditions, the reactions were usually stunned, silent amazement.

With the acoustic sensor mounted, Jas maneuvered the lifting boom to pick up Woody and prepare it for launch. In the edit bay, Morgan readied the ROV controls while Mateo sat beside him typing information into the control and measurement software for the acoustic imager. For once, I was able to sit back in one of the easy chairs and just watch. The two cameras mounted on *Water Horse*'s aft deck displayed two angles of the entire working area of the stern. Their images appeared in two windows on the monitor wall. Another window displayed the main camera from Woody. The center section of the monitor wall had been configured to display the acoustic imaging data, but now it just displayed black.

Morgan picked up a radio and called to Jas on the lifting boom. "Jas, we're ready to splash."

"Roger that. Splashing Woody."

We watched on the monitors as the lifting arm swung the ROV up and over the aft deck rail and began lowering the remote vehicle into the water. The ROV camera displayed the water's surface as it came closer and closer then submerged, transforming our view to one of clear blue watery scenes from below.

As soon as the ROV completely submerged, the acoustic sensors began transmitting bright color changes on the center window of the monitor wall. Mateo typed and clicked on the laptop, preparing to capture readings. "I am setting the sensors for a depth of twenty feet from the bottom. When the ROV reaches that depth, we'll see a clearer picture profile on the screen."

As Woody approached fifty feet from the surface, the acoustic imaging window solidified and began displaying pictures that looked similar to watching thermal images, with different shapes and colors morphing into one another.

"For you to better understand what you are seeing, hard-packed ocean bottom will appear as deep blue. As the bottom becomes less dense, the color will become green. Even less dense or loose bottom sand, yellow, and completely hollow spaces or underground caverns will display as black."

"What's the scale of the scan we're seeing on the screen?" I asked.

"The sensor is scanning an area about thirty yards across as it moves across the bottom," Mateo said.

As the ROV approached the edge of the search area, the colors on the screen transformed from deep blue to light blue and green. As Woody glided into the heart of the search zone, the colors changed from green to yellow with small veins of black flashing in and out of the colored-shaded areas. When the ROV came within one hundred yards of the cavern, we discovered the veins of black expanded and revealed pocket after pocket of hollow caverns and spaces under the sandy bottom. For the next hour, Morgan steered Woody across the entire search area and the results were the same: loose and uncompacted bottom and a network of partially filled tunnels and domes hidden under the surface.

"Have any thoughts, Mateo?"

"I know that there are many limestone caverns across the Gulf, but I've never seen research of caverns on this scale. These formations and the lithium we found in the bottom samples clearly point to something different going on here geologically."

"Could a cavern this size swallow up an entire island?" I asked.

Mateo thought silently, then said, "Yes, I think it could. But it would need a catalyst, like . . . an earthquake, perhaps."

"When was the last time an earthquake was recorded in the Gulf?" Morgan asked.

"There are tiny tremors from time to time, but nothing strong enough to cause this. In 2005, a 5.2 quake was centered three hundred fifty miles southwest of Tampa, but Bermeja was already missing by then."

Morgan radioed Jas. "Jas, Woody is headed for the surface, will you and Beau recover him?"

"We're standing ready," she answered.

My brain was spinning and continued to turn over and over on the rusted metal ring I found and the steel rail in the cavern. Seismographs around the world would detect an earthquake. A bomb would be even more obvious in this age of surveillance. What kind of catalyst could open up a cavern to swallow an entire island, but go undetected? Again, my far-fetched theory popped back into my head, but I still kept it to myself. So the three of us sat there, silently staring at the screens, even though there was nothing more to see on them.

"Boys, there's enough heat and smoke coming off your heads, you look like a couple of '73 Buicks with froze-up thermostats. Come on up to the galley. I got just the thing for overheated brains."

It was Rudy, doing a . . . Rudy thing.

"How does he do that?" I asked Morgan.

"Why do you keep questioning the Rudy juju?" Morgan

said, giving the back of my head an upward smack as he stood to leave.

"What is this . . . 'froze-up thermostat'?" Mateo asked, looking very confused.

"Lost in southern translation, my friend. Let's eat," I said, pointing him to the galley.

Chapter 12

THERE'S A HANDFUL OF THINGS aboard a ship that every sailor takes very seriously. One. Water must stay on the proper side of the hull—the outside. Two. Aboard any ship, fire is bad. Three. The captain will swiftly put a chronically surly shipmate ashore if they feel charitable or cut them adrift in a lifeboat if said sailor pushes their luck. And four, food. A well fed and amply watered crew will answer the bell for every watch and follow their captain into hell.

Tonight was certainly no exception aboard *Water Horse*. Rudy had prepared an enormous pan of lasagna that looked a foot deep. Thickly rich cheese was beautifully browned to perfection on top and the smell had the crazed looking crew drooling as they all sat like awaiting jackals. There was a mounded bowl of freshly cut and buttered French bread and a tub of mixed green salad large enough for an army.

After opening a bottle of red wine, I held it up, polling for takers, and hands went up. Glasses filled, we all sat, and I raised mine. "I'd like to once again welcome our new friend Dr. Mateo Cruz to the Water Horse family table. And to our newest member of the crew, seaman first class Harper."

"Hear! Hear!"

The meal was superb. We all passed dishes back and forth and again for seconds. Laughter filled the galley with old, re-peated stories you never minded hearing again and again. Mateo laughed along with the inside jokes, like he'd always been part of the team. When nothing but empty plates and overstuffed stomachs remained, I said, "We're heading for the coordinates of Isla Escondida first thing tomorrow morn-ing, so everyone try to get some sleep."

"It looks to be a five-and-a-half-hour run to those coordi-nates," Jerry said.

"I'll make sure everything is stowed and ready for run-ning before I hit the rack," Beau said.

"I'll give you a hand," Jas added.

"We're going to post a watch tonight," I said. "I'll take the first shift. Will someone relieve me at midnight?"

Volunteers spoke up around the table until the watch schedule filled, with no need for assignments to be made.

Everyone thanked Rudy for the evening feast, and with "good nights" from all, the crew ambled off to awaiting bunks.

After repeated protests, I won the tug-of-war with Rudy to clean up the mess. And after several motherly instructions for where things should go after washing and drying, I finally convinced him and Harper to retire.

With the galley shipshape, I stepped out on the main deck to another beautiful night on the Gulf. The weather was holding well for us, with flat calm seas, light breeze, and no rain. The Milky Way lit the dark sky, and with temps in the seventies, it made being on watch anything but a chore.

I walked up the side deck to the bow and found Jas taking in the evening as well.

"You better get some rack time while you can," I said.

"I will, just soaking up some of this," she said, raising her face and arms to the glow of starlight as it sparkled off the rippled water stretching to the horizon in every direction.

"Never gets old, does it?" I said.

Staring up into the night glow, she said, "It doesn't for me."

"Hey, Rudy told me you almost set a new world record on your last free-dive event."

"Came within two meters," she said, smiling.

"Ever think about going back and finishing that?"

"I do sometimes. It got a little complicated. And for now, I really like what we do here."

"Me too. You know, ahh, yesterday, with you and the sinkhole." The lump in my throat felt the size of a baseball. "It scared me. I thought I might—I thought we might lose you."

Jas turned and looked at me. She smiled and tilted her head, then approached me and put a warm hand on my arm. "Michael, Neptune will need to work much harder than that to get me off your boat."

"I-I'm very glad to hear that," I said. And the tinny notes of chopsticks plinked quietly on my toy piano.

Jas stood, still smiling up at me. "Good night, Michael."

"Night, Jas."

I had almost given up on sleep, two hours after Jerry relieved me at midnight. I had finally just drifted off when the knock on my cabin door woke me, and I sprang to my feet, completely awake.

Rudy was my middle of the night knocker. "Cap, hate to wake you, but something's up."

As I opened the door, I could immediately hear Harper barking. "What going on?"

"It's Harper. He heard something and has been running

up and down the side decks barking and snarling at the water."

I followed him to the main deck, where I found Morgan with a Mossberg 12-gauge in his right hand. He was watching Harper, who stood with his front paws on the side rail of the starboard bow, growling and barking at the water with every wiry gray hair along his backbone raised. Rudy had powered up the new underwater lights and his description was accurate. The supernova of light emitting from the hull below our waterline lit up the water for twenty yards in every direction.

"We're gonna blind the fish," I said.

"Pretty impressive, huh?" Rudy said, smiling.

"Thoughts?" I asked Morgan, who stood staring into the glow of the water.

"Harper certainly heard something. Look at him."

"All right, Harper, that's enough," Rudy called.

Reluctantly, the barking stopped, but as Harper approached us, the low frequency of his growl motor bubbled from his chest and every gray hair remained on alert.

"Good job, Harper," I said as I gave him a head scratch.

His tail wagged, thumping the gunnel of the side deck, but he didn't give up the grrrr.

"I'm gonna get wet and look around," Morgan said.

"There'll be no sleeping now, let's go," I answered.

Ten minutes later, Morgan and I glided under the hull of *Water Horse*, with the underwater lights shining on us like we were on a concert stage.

"Rudy never does anything halfway," Morgan said into his coms.

"No, but do we need this much?" I asked.

Something caught Morgan's attention, and he spun and drifted upside down against the hull. Twenty feet aft of our bulbous bow, he reached and touched something against the steel. "The lights might be perfect for situations just like tonight," Morgan said, as he removed a small object from the hull about the size of a computer mouse. It was obviously magnetic, and it had a tiny antenna protruding from the front.

"A tracker?" I asked.

"Won't know for sure until we crack it open, but looks like one."

Morgan tucked the black puck looking device in a pocket on his dive vest and we both started a meticulous search of every inch of our hull. Forty-five minutes later, we surfaced near the boarding platform. Jas and Beau gave us a hand out of the water. We weren't even out of our gear before Jas asked, "Anything?"

Morgan pulled the object from his vest pocket and tossed it to her. She held it up, turning it a few times for a better look. "Tracker?" she asked.

"Let's get it on the bench and find out," Morgan said.

Jas spun and headed for the camera shop.

"How'd they get that close without anyone hearing or seeing them on the radar?" Beau asked.

"If they came in on a small inflatable and swam in the last mile, it wouldn't be hard," Morgan replied.

Jerry came out onto the aft deck and joined our trio. "Captain, I had the radar set to twelve miles, because I was watching for any shipping traffic. It never occurred to me that someone may swim up in the middle of the Gulf."

"None of us did, Jerry. It's okay."

"Glad Harper sensed them," he said.

"Yeah, he's definitely earned his rations already."

In the camera shop, Jas had the small device on the work-table split apart like an oyster.

"What do we have?" Morgan asked.

"It's definitely a tracker. A good one, satellite based," Jas answered. "I kept the battery connected, so whoever is tracking us will think it's still in place."

Mateo entered the camera shop and looked over Jas's shoulder at the tracker lying split apart on the bench.

"A satellite tracker?" he asked.

"It's safe to say that someone isn't buying our 'fish counting' cover story," I said.

Morgan said, "I'm beginning to feel like a lot of people are watching us, and I don't like it. Dr. Cruz, does that look like CISEN tech to you?"

Mateo reached and carefully picked up the two halves of the device. "No, this looks more advanced than the trackers I've seen used in the field."

I said, "I think we should move on to the site of Isla Escondida. Any objections, Dr. Cruz?"

"If more people are monitoring us, we probably should move faster," he answered.

"Agreed. Let's pull the hook and get underway. Beau, can you take the first helm watch?"

"Absolutely."

"We've already set the coordinates in the chart plotter. We're about one hundred thirty kilometers west of that destination. As a precaution, let's run AIS dark," I said.

The AIS beacon identified our vessel and our position to other boats in the vicinity. It was an important safety measure, especially for large cargo and passenger ships, aiding in early detection and collision avoidance. For now, we would bend the rules and stay unidentified, even though radar would easily detect us as an unnamed target.

"Jas, put that tracker back together and meet me on the aft deck," Morgan said.

Jas went to work reassembling the tracker, and I followed Morgan out of the camera shop. Out on deck, Morgan opened one of the storage lockers on the stern and pulled out a small buoy about twelve inches in circumference, a coil of lightweight line, and a small lead weight as large as his fist. Jas stepped up as Morgan finished tying the line to the buoy and the lead weight to the end of the line. Jas, anticipating what Morgan was thinking, had already attached a strong adhesive tab to the bottom of the tracker as she handed it to Morgan. He stuck the tracker to the buoy, walked to the rail, and dropped the line and anchor over, followed by the buoy.

Morgan said, "Probably won't fool them for long, but let's let them think we're sitting right here as long as we can."

"I like it," I said, and unclipped the radio from my belt. "Jerry, will you man the windlass? Let's pull the hook and get underway."

"Roger that, Cap."

The new underwater lights powered down, and I felt the big Caterpillar main engine start, as Rudy was already in the loop. That familiar thrum of the *Water Horse* power plant vibrating under foot was a great feeling. The seas were still flat and the light of the quarter moon mixed with the stars would make for perfect predawn running.

I keyed the mic on the radio. "Beau, once we secure the

anchor, let's take it nice and slow, say eight knots. We'll just make like an old shrimp boat heading east."

"Eight knots, roger that. I make a helluva shrimp boat captain."

We'd have a few hours of running before sunrise, then five to six hours in daylight, with the entire run taking eight hours at our lower than normal cruising speed. I didn't have many illusions about fooling anyone long term, but the decoy tracker, no AIS, and a slower radar target might buy us a little time without anyone looking for us.

Sunrise peeked over the eastern horizon at half past six. Early morning light streaked across the watery expanse, creating millions of twinkling stars that stretched to the horizon as it reflected off the small ripples. The water was such a beautiful blue-green that the good Lord probably smiled to himself as he painted this unique hue that has delighted Gulf sailors for centuries.

Our weather forecast called for continued fair weather, so that was good news. We just needed to find a few more corner and edge pieces for our puzzle. Pieces we had. Pieces with limestone caverns, traces of lithium, steel industrial parts—where they shouldn't be. Add to that, a big barrel of players with financial motivation for mischief. But how all those pieces went together was a mess. They were all piled on the table with the gray, no picture side, facing up.

The morning progressed uneventfully as we chugged eastward. Just before noon, I stepped into the pilothouse. *Water Horse* was three miles from our destination, and Jerry was at the helm.

"We getting close, Jerry?"

"We are, Cap. Just a few miles. But take a look at this."

Jerry pointed to the radar screen at a large target fifteen miles east-southeast of our position.

"Pretty big boat," I said.

"Looks like he's sitting just off one of those small atolls, anchored maybe."

"Put a radar target on her. I want to know if she moves."

"Roger that."

As we reached our coordinates, Jerry slowed the boat, and I radioed Beau. "Let's get ready to drop the hook."

Jerry brought our forward progress to a stop, and I gave Beau a hand signal for the drop. Seconds later, twenty-five hundred pounds of steel connected to one inch chain spilled from the anchor locker and dropped eighty feet to the sandy bottom, where another small island was supposed to be.

Morgan stepped into the pilothouse just as the ship's VHF radio squawked to life. "*Water Horse, Water Horse, Water Horse, Voltaic.*"

Chapter 13

MORGAN AND I LOOKED AT EACH OTHER for a few long seconds and I pulled the radio mic and answered, "*Voltaic*, this is *Water Horse*, go ahead."

"*Water Horse,* switch and answer six-eight."

"Six-eight, over." I switched the VHF radio to a talk channel, and the call came back. "*Water Horse, Voltaic*."

"*Water Horse*, go ahead," I answered.

"Hey boys, it's Sims. Is your old squid of a brother around?"

I looked at Morgan, eyebrows raised and held the mic in his direction. He hesitated a long moment and reached to take the mic. "What's up, you overgrown mongrel?"

"Hey, brother! We're anchored up off an atoll about eighty miles off Progreso. You guys anywhere near the area? I'd love to treat you both to a dinner far too nice for two swabbies like you."

Morgan looked at me, and I shrugged my shoulders in a nonanswer. "Give me your position," Morgan said.

Sims read off his position, and I wrote it on the notepad laying on the chart table. Morgan stalled while I worked out his position on the chart. Morgan said, "What in the world are you guys doing out here in the middle of the Gulf?"

I pinpointed Sims's position on the chart and stepped over to the radar, and pointed to the large target fifteen miles from our position, as Sims answered, "Are you kidding? My client has his own private beach, all the comforts of home and no one around for hundreds of miles."

"Roger that," Morgan said.

"If it's not too far, you two take a tender and come break some bread. The boss says it's okay, and he'd even like to meet you."

"Let me plot your position on the chart and I'll ring you back."

"Don't wait too long. The chef is preparing lobster tonight."

"You're right at home, aren't you, Sims?"

"Don't you know it, brother."

Morgan hung the mic against the radio and looked at me. "Whaddya think?"

"If we were out here actually counting fish, I'd say you and I hit the jackpot for a great free meal and night on a nice boat. But with all the events and discoveries of the last two days, we just aren't that lucky," I said.

"Agreed, we are not. But if we go for dinner, we're going with more than just a bottle of wine for our host."

"After seeing Sims grab that guy in the bar, do you have a bazooka on board?" I asked.

Morgan laughed. "He's not that big."

I shrugged and shook my head. He seemed pretty damned big to me.

Morgan made the call to Sims and accepted his invitation. They agreed on eight p.m. so we'd be able to dive the site we were on and collect additional bottom samples before we'd have to leave. I asked Jerry to help me pull our twenty-six-foot RIB from the upper deck and prepare it for our run to the dinner date. The rest of the team was already busy pre-paring for another dive as soon as we could get wet.

At two p.m., Jas, Mateo, and I sat on the aft deck benches, doing final checks on our gear.

"Heads on a swivel down there, okay?" I said.

"Understood," Jas answered.

"We will only need a handful of samples," Mateo said.

"If anyone spots anything unusual, call out on coms immediately and stop," I said.

Heads nodded, and we stood to get into position on the boarding platform. Mateo and Jas splashed first, and I followed, then resurfaced for Beau to hand me the underwater camera housing. As I resubmerged, I pulled the record trigger to capture footage of our descent to the bottom eighty feet below. Once I reached the bottom, I continued recording. The sandy contours looked almost identical to the previous site. But as I glided over the flat landscape, into the center of the search area, I saw small shallow craters, much like the beds a female fish creates to lay her eggs. Mateo and Jas were already busy collecting samples, and Woody was gliding over the site as well. The crew kept the acoustic imaging module configuration on the ROV to image any subterranean caverns. We were all betting on finding similar structures on this site and within minutes, Morgan's voice came over the coms. "Hey guys, I'm seeing very similar caverns on the acoustic imager to what we saw at the last site. I'm recording it all, so the doctor can analyze it, but it sure looks the same to these untrained eyes."

Mateo looked over at me and nodded.

The small depressions didn't seem to have any pattern in their placements, and there were no fish tending to any of them. But they seemed almost natural occurrences on the bottom. I was beginning to see why previous surveys of the area found nothing unusual about the sites. As I continued to glide over the bottom, recording video, a glint of light flashed on the rear viewfinder of the camera and caught my eye, causing me to stop. I exhaled and gently allowed myself to descend to the bottom. My knees gently settled in the sand. Two feet in front of me, I could see what the camera sensor had captured. It was another small depression in the sand, but this one had a very thin metallic wire stretched across it. I froze.

I spoke, engaging the coms in my mask. "Jas, Mateo . . . Freeze!"

I carefully turned to my left and saw the pair, thirty yards away. Mateo had just inserted his sample probe into the sand.

"Mateo, gently take your hand off the probe." He released the probe and both of them looked back at me. "Both of you head to the surface, now. Morgan, recall Woody and get him back on deck."

"Roger that, but are you okay?"

"What's up?" Jas asked.

"I'm not sure yet, but I don't want to take any chances. You two head up and I'll be right behind you."

Jas and Mateo began slowly ascending, and I turned back to the depression and the wire. Carefully, I clipped the camera housing to the rear side of my vest and eased a little closer. I gently fanned the sand away from the spot where the exposed wire vanished under the sand. I felt a presence to my right, and I turned to see Jas glide up next to me. "I told you to head to the surface."

"And I'm not leaving you here alone," she said forcefully. Seconds later, Mateo drifted next to Jas.

"Neither will I," Mateo said.

I could see the resolve in both their eyes, so resigned, I said, "Stay off the bottom and don't touch anything." I pointed out the wire stretched across the depression. They both stared at the wire and floated silently.

"Still want to stay?" I asked. Mateo tentatively nodded.

Jas said, "Bring it, Neptune."

I smiled, then continued my very gentle fanning. I waved away sand from two more feet of wire before I saw the thin strand terminate into a small disc shape that appeared anchored to the bottom.

"Damn, I was afraid of that," I said as I reached for the camera. When the sand settled enough, I snapped a half dozen pictures of what seemed like a small explosive charge.

"Someone doesn't want us exploring this site," Mateo said.

"I wonder why there was nothing like this at the other site," Jas said.

"Maybe now, we're getting too close," I answered.

Jas touched my arm and pointed to another depression about twelve feet ahead of where I knelt on the bottom. "Look, isn't that another wire?"

The light glinted across the wire, now making it easier to see.

"Let's get topside," I said.

Careful not to disturb the bottom, we added a bit of air to our BC vests to increase our buoyancy and ascended off the bottom ten feet until I felt we were far enough away to give gentle kicks with our fins.

Back on deck, Morgan was busy removing the acoustic sensor from Woody. I called him over to the bench and showed him pictures of the disc charge I had photographed on the bottom. "It's a charge all right. I've used similar ones on a few missions. You're lucky. One small tug on that wire and you'd been fish food."

"That's encouraging. Is it dangerous to us on the surface?"

"No, probably not. The concussion would make a two-foot-deep hole in the sand and turn the insides of anything alive to jelly for thirty feet in any direction."

"Oh, is that all?" I said.

"Why put explosive charges on this site?" Jas asked.

"My guess is that whoever is behind this doesn't want anyone stumbling across subterranean caverns and industrial equipment where it shouldn't be," I answered.

"It doesn't seem to be a well-kept secret that we're out here," Morgan said. "Perhaps when they saw how long we explored the Bermeja site, they felt they couldn't take any chances on this site."

"Maybe our dinner host has seen some unusual activity out here in the Gulf. Should we ask him?" I said.

"You can count on it. Hey, I want to send Woody on another dive. Give me a hand."

Morgan retrieved a section of line from the locker. It had a lead weight on the end and he attached two more small square weights about the size of a pack of cigarettes to the line at two-foot intervals from the end of the line. Then he secured the opposite end of the line to Woody. "Help me get him launched," he said.

I manned the lifting boom and picked up the ROV and maneuvered it to the rail as Morgan carefully walked alongside, keeping the weighted line coiled and ready to release into the water. It would trail behind as Woody descended to the bottom. When I had the ROV positioned over the surface and clear of the stern, I yelled to Morgan, "Ready?"

Morgan nodded. I released Woody from the arm and Morgan threw the line in a way that made it uncoil far behind Woody's front end. Morgan, Jas, Mateo, and I headed to the edit bay where Morgan could pilot the ROV and we could observe on the cameras. Woody would make the first part of the trip autonomously, then Morgan would take over. As we reached the cabin, we could already see the bottom approaching on the large monitors as the cameras captured the descent. At thirty feet from the bottom, Woody stopped its dive and hovered, awaiting Morgan's control.

Morgan sat behind the joysticks and restarted the trip toward the bottom. As the ROV went deeper, we could make out the small depressions in the sand.

"See right there?" I pointed to a spot on the monitor. "That's where we found one of the charges, in one of the depressions."

Morgan expertly positioned the ROV so that the weights on the end of the line lay on the bottom. Then he steered Woody across a corner of the search area that contained more small craters. We watched closely as the weighted line dragged across the sandy bottom, leaving a cloudy trail of swirling sand and silt. Twenty seconds into the trek, the rear-facing camera on the ROV captured the weights dipping down into one of the depressions. A silent flash filled the screen for a split second, followed by a small fireball from an explosion. The water around the blast created a bubble two feet across, and the bottom sand exploded outward. The concussion reached the ROV, and it tumbled over in the water several times and the view on the monitor made us almost too dizzy to watch. After a few seconds, the spinning stopped and the ROV's view stabilized. Morgan's estimates were correct. As the sand settled and the water clarity returned, the camera revealed a two-foot-deep hole in the sand, sixty feet from where Woody now hovered, capturing it all.

"*¡Ay, carajo!*" Mateo muttered.

"Well, that would've sucked," I said.

"It'd been over quick." Morgan laughed.

"Mateo, can you and Jas run the few samples you collected and see if there're traces of lithium on this site as well?"

"Right away, Captain."

The ship-wide speaker sounded and Jerry's voice filled the space. "Captain, we've got more visitors headed this way."

Chapter 14

ON THE WING DECK of the pilothouse, I raised the binoculars to the southern horizon. Seconds later, a small speck appeared out on the edge of my visibility. Rudy entered the pilothouse with Harper and stepped up behind me. "Just never thought the middle of the Gulf would be this popular a spot."

"You and me both," I said.

"Any idea who it is?" he asked.

"Not a clue, but there're way too many people that know how to find us for my tastes."

I looked through the binoculars again and could now see it was a military launch.

Jerry, still on watch, picked up a handheld radio and

called out, "Hey Beau, we've got more visitors headed our way. Can you rig some lines and bumpers for our guests?"

"You got it," Beau answered.

Harper stood close, almost against my leg. My right thigh vibrated as Harper's inaudible, low growl rumbled deep in his chest as he too looked out at the approaching boat.

"What's got his dander up?" I asked Rudy.

"Beats me, Cap, but his track record isn't bad so far."

Another glance through the glasses and I could see two enlisted military figures and none other than the Mexican Secretary of Energy, Mariana Vega.

"Well, I'll be damned," I said.

"Who is it?" Rudy asked.

"Our client."

Ten minutes later, I stood on the aft deck with Morgan and Dr. Cruz. Rudy stood just outside the cabin door on the aft deck, with Harper alongside, who was now openly growling at the approaching boat. I looked back at the two of them and said, "I think you two better stay below for this. No need to maul the client just yet."

"Roger that, Cap. Let's go, Harper. We'll get you some-one to maul later." And they disappeared through the hatch.

Beau and Jas caught lines as the thirty-six-foot military launch pulled up against our stern on the starboard side. The two soldiers stayed aboard the launch as Beau extended a hand, helping Ms. Vega onto the platform and up the boarding steps. Even though she must have just experienced a two-plus-hour high-speed run out into the Gulf, she once again was impeccably dressed in a dark gray business suit with modest, but still high, heels. I approached as our guest stepped onto the deck. "Welcome aboard the *Water Horse*, Secretary Vega."

"Thank you, Captain."

"How did you know we were here and to what do we owe this unexpected visit?"

"I heard that a petty officer met you to recover some evidence concerning a missing vessel and I knew the coordinates for Isla Escondida. I'm quite resourceful, Captain Gannon. But now, it's my turn. When we hired your team, I thought I was clear about my need to have constant and timely updates on your progress."

"Yes, ma'am, you were."

She waited, head slightly tilted, expecting an answer.

Dr. Cruz answered for me. "Secretary Vega, it is all my fault. I asked the captain to delay some of our updates to you until we had something more conclusive to report."

"Dr. Cruz, you do not have the authority to make such a recommendation and I am most certain you and your department are not writing the checks for this operation."

"No, Secretary . . . I do not."

The heat did not subside, so I interjected. "Why don't we all walk up to the galley, sit, and we'll give you a progress report right now?"

Easing her intensity slightly, the secretary said, "That would be satisfactory."

The four of us filed up the side deck, up one set of steps, and through the passageway into the galley. Because he was always anticipating, Rudy had started a pot of coffee and had mugs ready to go. We sat around the table and I began betting that Mateo would follow my lead.

"Secretary Vega, our team made two extensive dives on the previous recorded site of Bermeja. We recorded video footage and photographs of the area and collected numerous sea bottom samples across a broad area within and around the coordinates. The area did not appear to be disturbed or have any characteristics uncommon with that known area of the Gulf." Mateo's affirmative nods were supportive and convincing.

Ms. Vega nodded and smiled. "So just as my colleagues and I expected."

"Largely, yes. We only arrived at this site this morning, so we'd just completed our first dive before you arrived. So far, this site appears to be the same as the site of Bermeja in every way, although we are early in our observations and testing."

Ms. Vega seemed very confident as she continued nodding along. "So we can put to rest any rumors of the American CIA blowing up islands, yes?"

"We could confidently say that at this time, yes," Mateo said.

I needed to see if I could create a crack in the government official's Teflon facade, so I took a chance. "The samples of the bottom sand on the first site and"—I looked at Mateo for confirmation, and he nodded—"and this site contained significant traces of a substance we didn't expect."

Ms. Vega's expression changed, but only slightly. "Yes, and what was the substance you found?"

"The seafloor of both the site of Bermeja and the site of Isla Escondida contained significant traces of lithium."

That changed her face. The smiled vanished. "Lithium?"

"Yes, Secretary."

"The type of lithium extracted and used in the manufacturing of electric vehicle batteries?"

"The very same," I said.

"How unusual," she said. "We have not been made aware of any significant amounts of lithium in the waters of the Gulf of Mexico. Dr. Cruz, have you any knowledge of lithium being discovered in our waters?"

"No, Secretary, I do not."

The secretary rose and looked at her watch. "These are

significant findings. I need to report this to the rest of the task force right away."

"Do you have any other questions for us at this time, Secretary Vega?" I asked.

"No, Captain. You are doing excellent work. I trust you and Dr. Cruz will complete your thorough search of this site and prepare a complete report for our agency."

"Of course, Secretary Vega. We certainly will."

Mateo added, "Our data will be very useful to our government moving forward, Secretary. It is very important work."

Ms. Vega was already on the move toward the aft deck as she said, "Yes, Dr. Cruz, please keep me updated on your findings. We look forward to your final reports."

We followed along behind her, and I gave Mateo a quizzical look. He shrugged, and we continued to trail behind the quick clicking of the secretary's heels along *Water Horse*'s steel decks. When we reached the stern, she turned and extended her hand to me. "Captain Gannon, thank you for your hospitality and thorough work. Dr. Cruz, thank you for your service to Mexico. I will be in touch." And with that, the Secretary of Energy boarded the military launch, and with some rapid and curt instructions from the secretary in Spanish, the soldiers hurriedly cast off the lines and pushed the throttles to the stops, speeding toward the southern horizon.

"That was a weird meeting," Morgan said.

I nodded in agreement. "The mention of the lithium certainly seemed to rattle her."

"Yes, the secretary was not aware of lithium's presence in the Gulf. If the Ministry of Energy knew it was here, they would be trying to extract it as we speak," Mateo said.

My phone rang, and I looked at the screen. "It's El," I said. "This may be informative." I put the phone on speaker and answered the call. "Hey there, got any news?"

"A cold is what I've got." She sounded awful.

"I'm sorry."

"Don't even tell me what the temperature is there today."

"I will not," I said.

"Okay, here is what I have for you. Goddard Petroleum, like I said before, is new to the game and they've been throwing around a tremendous amount of cash, trying to buy some credibility in oil exploration. It's been working for them so far. Their stock is up almost thirty percent in the last twelve months. It looks like they've done several big hush-hush contracts with a company called Fayhee Energy, out of Austin, Texas. They seem to be experimenting with fringe techniques in oil exploration by using unconventional methods that were all long shots. But they've scored enough successes, it makes them attractive to a company like Goddard. The Fayhee Energy CEO is a hot shot MIT engineering grad named Carl

Fayhee, who has sold a handful of energy extraction patents for millions in the last ten years. He owns one of the most advanced and expensive superyachts ever built."

I looked at Morgan and he hung his head and quietly muttered, "Dammit . . . Sims."

I let that set in for a second and then continued. "Well, oddly enough, they have invited your other brother and me aboard the *Voltaic*, the Fayhee corporate yacht, this evening for a lobster dinner." The line stayed silent for several long seconds.

"I really do hate you both quite a bit right now."

"Come on, sis, don't be a hater," Morgan said.

"It's twenty-one degrees here right now and I have enough Vicks Vapor Rub on my chest that my pajamas are sticking. Maybe it's closer to loathing." She blew her nose like a trumpet. "Listen, there is way more going on here than we know yet. You two should watch your backs. The amount of potential money on the line makes people do really stupid things."

I said, "El, we've found significant traces of lithium on this site as well."

"The lithium is interesting, but I don't know how it fits in just yet. I know Fayhee Energy is responsible for discovering some sources for it in the past—ah-choo!"

"Salud!" Mateo said.

"Thank you. Was that by any chance, Mr. Muscles and Smiles?"

"It was." I laughed. "Ellie, meet Dr. Mateo Cruz, a new friend."

"I hope you feel much better soon, señora Ellie," Mateo said.

"Thank you, Dr. Cruz. Let me see if Fayhee used any new tech in the discovery of their previous lithium finds. But no kidding, you boys, be careful. Oil money is a whole new kind of greed."

"Understood," I said. "Feel better, okay? And I'll fly you down as soon as we wrap this up."

"I'm already packed." And she ended the call.

Morgan looked at me and said, "Looks like we need to get ready for our dinner date and we're not going empty-handed. Let's have Beau and Jas meet you and me down in my locker in ten minutes."

"That sounds ominous," I said.

"Nah, that sounds fun!"

Mateo looked on, a little confused. Morgan tried to fill in some gaps. "Dr. Cruz, you mentioned in the beginning of our new understanding together that we had CISEN's approval to employ our operational . . . preferences, correct?"

"Yes, completely," Mateo answered.

"See, brother—fun."

Down in Morgan's "locker," that anyone would call a very well-equipped modern armory, Morgan, Jas, Beau, and I stood around the worktable and a laptop that displayed a promotional wide shot of the new luxury yacht, *Voltaic*.

"Okay, team. According to my old buddy Sims, the *Voltaic* is a three-hundred-eighty-foot yacht that's out here anchored off an atoll in proximity to some strange events and a booby-trapped section of ocean bottom, where an island should be. Add to that, the shot up tender we recovered and the remains of the *Coral Explorer*. My bet is that these guys are up to no good."

"You seem convinced that Fayhee, Sims, or both are involved in all of this," Beau said.

"It's been bothering me since we saw him in Cancun," Morgan answered. "If you need corporate security and privacy, you hire big goons that are cheap and look good. They're great for crowd control and keeping the press pushed back. If you need something broken, blown up, or vanished, you hire someone with the skills of a Sims."

"You think Sims is capable of flipping from a good guy to a bad guy?" Jas asked.

"I think Sims was trained and honed as a warrior. There's not much room in your brain for anything else when your deployed. When you take the battle away, a lot of guys struggle with that and lose their way. A battle is a battle. Sims skills alone make him a dangerous man, so we will not underestimate him."

"What kind of security team do you think Sims has on board?" I asked.

"They'll be good, but probably not smart. Sims always had a hard time with people smarter than him. So if he put the team together, he'll want to be the top dog. But you and I are going to just be charming and enjoy the evening. I think the real business is going to be under the waterline. We need to take a look under that beast of a boat."

"How we gonna do that?" Beau asked.

"Easy," Morgan said. "You and Jas are going to look."

Chapter 15

At six thirty, five of us, plus Harper, stood on the aft deck around the RIB. The sun had already set, and we worked under the aft deck lights. A gentle breeze accented a beautiful night on the water. Beau stood inside the twenty-six-foot hull of the RIB, loading gear into the storage boxes in the boat's cockpit area. Harper, who was almost as tall as a man on his hind legs, stood with his front paws against the gunnel watching the loading action. His hanging tongue and twitching ears clearly indicated hope for a turn to be hoisted into the boat.

"You can't make this run, buddy. Someone needs to keep an eye on Rudy," I said.

"He's a traitor." Rudy laughed, as he stood by on the controls of the lifting boom, thirty feet away.

Morgan had assembled two rebreather units for our two divers to prevent leaving any exhalation bubbles that might be detected on the surface. He also included two personal underwater propulsion systems and infrared night vision goggles, adapted for their masks. Jas was already in her tropical wet suit and tactical vest. Beau, Morgan, and I dressed in nicer cargo pants and Water Horse golf shirts. I handed two night-vision-equipped underwater camera housings up to Beau and he stowed them. Then Morgan handed him two Heckler & Koch HK416 compact rifles. The former marine took the weapons one by one, checked the slides and mags and stowed them in a concealed area under the center console. Morgan designed and built the two small compartments for the RIB on our passage from Alaska. When closed, they appeared to be typical wire chase channels under the console area.

Morgan and I didn't know if we'd be checked for weapons, but regardless, we both wore Springfield Armory XD-S 9mms in concealed waist holsters in the waist of our cargo pants. When the team completed final checks and cross checks of the gear, the four of us climbed into the RIB and I gave Rudy the sign to splash us.

The boom lifted our military looking black-and-gray craft off the deck and Rudy eased us over the stern rail. Harper, clearly protesting his absence from the away party, barked and made circles on the deck. We touched the water and the hoist lines slackened enough for Morgan and me to release the snap rings from the lifting eyes. I keyed the handheld radio mic. "We're clear, Rudy. Beau and Jas will be on coms."

"Got ya, Cap. You guys be careful out there."

"See you in a few hours," I answered.

Beau pushed the throttles forward on the twin one-hundred-fifty-horse motors, and the big four strokes gave a throaty growl as they dug a hole in the water and quickly popped us up on plane. Within seconds, we sped across the flat, calm water at forty knots.

Nine miles from the coordinates of the *Voltaic*, Beau throttled back to idle speed and turned to Jas. "You ready to crawl in your box?"

"Yeah, but don't get cute, or you'll find yourself swimming back to the boat."

"It was an innocent question."

Jas punched Beau in the arm on her way aft to the remaining empty storage box in the cockpit. Before she stepped into the box, she removed her Sig P365 and snuck the slide back for a peek at the loaded round and reholstered the weapon. I stepped up as she slid down into the fiberglass locker and handed her a bottled water. "Are you good for this?"

"Hell yes."

"Nothing crazy, right? Get in, look around, grab pictures of anything strange, and get back to the RIB," I said.

Jas put her hand on mine, which was resting on the side of the locker, and smiled up at me. That familiar rush of warmth shot up my arm and my mind started a second guessing game as to the recklessness of this whole idea. I didn't know how anyone could look so good folded like a pretzel into a storage locker, but somehow she did.

"I got this, Michael. You two are the ones probably going into the lion's den. Watch each other's backs, okay?"

"Always," I said. And I reluctantly shut the lid to the locker.

Beau buried the throttles again and in three minutes, the lights of the enormous luxury yacht, *Voltaic*, lit up the horizon in all directions as we closed on her position. It looked like we were heading for a small city as the illuminated windows of the five-decked monster loomed in the darkness like a small skyscraper. Beau made a wide sweeping turn around the yacht's port stern and pulled us up alongside the massive boarding platform that stretched across the entire stern. Two linebacker-sized crewmen wearing pressed khakis and starched short-sleeved dress shirts, complete with epaulets, met us formally as Beau gently put our starboard gunnel against the teak boarding deck. Morgan and I stepped effortlessly over onto their deck as if we were daily visitors to the *Voltaic*.

The larger of the two crewmen greeted us. "Good evening and welcome aboard, gentlemen. Our director of security and Mr. Fayhee are expecting you."

"Thank you," I replied. And I looked back at Beau and gave him a wink. "Mr. Benson, I'll phone the *Water Horse* when we're ready to return."

"Aye that, Captain Gannon, we'll be standing by."

Morgan rolled his eyes.

The two crewmen led the way across an expansive aft deck covered in flawlessly maintained teak decking and into an enormous salon beautifully appointed in fine furnishing and artwork. Once inside, soft jazz music filled the space. Not too loud but just . . . there. Sims emerged from a passageway, somewhere forward. "The Brothers Gannon! Welcome aboard the *Voltaic*. What do ya think, boys?"

Morgan stepped forward to shake his hand. "Thanks for having us, Sims. We were ready for a night out. This is a helluva ship."

"Ditto on both for me, Sims, thanks."

"Come on up to the lounge, Carl wants to meet you both."

"Carl?" Morgan asked, feigning ignorance of the name of our host.

"Sorry, Carl Fayhee, this is his boat. He's the CEO of Fayhee Energy."

We went up an impressive, curved mahogany and steel staircase to an equally impressive lounge area. Two more large and uniformed crewmen stood on the periphery of the space and a casually dressed man with black-rimmed, professor-type glasses sat in a comfortable chair with half-filled rocks glass.

"Carl, these are my friends Michael and Morgan Gannon, with Water Horse Expeditions."

The man stood, putting his drink on the side table. He had an awkward smile, a shaggy mop of dark hair, and a real Bill Gates vibe about him. But he seemed friendly enough as he crossed the room to greet us. "Nice to meet you both," he said.

"I'm Michael," I said, as we shook hands.

Fayhee extended his hand to my brother.

"Morgan. Thanks for having us, Mr. Fayhee."

"Carl, please," he said. "Would either of you like a drink?"

"A glass of anything you're pouring is fine," Morgan said.

Carl looked at me and I nodded. "The same will be perfect."

The man walked over to the well-stocked mahogany bar, large enough for a small nightclub, tonged a few cubes into two crystal-cut rocks glasses, and dispensed a pair of healthy pours from a similarly cut decanter. Handing us our drinks, he said to Morgan, "I understand you were on the Teams with Sims."

"I was," Morgan said.

In all the years that Morgan spent in the DEV Group Teams, that was as detailed an answer as I'd ever heard him give to that question.

Amused, Carl dug a little further. "Sims tells me you have quite a reputation. He says he's never met a better operator."

"Carl, by looking around, it's obvious you must be a very intelligent man. You're not actually listening to that meat-head, are you?"

Carl broke out laughing, and Sims hung and shook his head. Morgan just forced a small smile. "Come sit down, men. That's forty-year-old scotch you're drinking. You should enjoy it slowly," Carl said.

We all sat, and Sims took a barstool positioned just out-side the circle of easy chairs. Morgan sat facing Sims, and I sat facing the men standing on the edge of the lounge. I glanced at my watch. Beau and Jas should have reached their splash point by now. The plan was for Beau to run the RIB back in the direction of *Water Horse*. Once over the horizon, they'd drop an anchor. Jas would emerge from her hide, Beau would suit up, and the two would use the personal propulsion rigs to power back to *Voltaic*'s position. The pair would survey the area around and under the superyacht, using the infrared night vision goggles and night-vision-equipped cameras. We agreed on a strict thirty-minute time limit to recon the area and then power straight back to the RIB and await our call for pickup.

"Michael, what can you tell us about your current survey work for the Mexican government?"

"Not much to tell, really. There's been some concern about the health of the sport fishing industry off the peninsula. We've been doing some surveys and species count out on the edge of the shelf and now we're looking at some of the species that use the shallow water around the atolls as spawning ground."

Carl smiled and nodded with an air of interest. "I see. They do take their fishing very seriously down here. Have you ever done any oil exploration work?"

"No, that's a little out of my area of expertise. I'm primarily a videographer and photographer. Our clients usually handle the hard science. But no. Nothing in oil exploration so far. We're still a young company."

Yet another thick-necked crewman entered the lounge. "Mr. Fayhee, the chef is ready to serve dinner."

Carl stood, and we mirrored him. "Let's pick this up over dinner."

We followed our host to the dining room, which was

down one deck and forward of the opulent salon. More crisp uniforms, now on a team of female stewards, stood ready around the large, elaborately set table. Our drinks were refreshed, and small talked filled the room as we got settled. Carl gave us a brief history of the boat. The *Voltaic* was constructed in the renown Feadship shipyards in the Netherlands. Her three-hundred-eighty-foot hull had additional plating, giving the ship ice-breaking ability. It was powered by an experimental hydrogen propulsion system that, accompanied with a sincere apology, made it impossible for a tour of the engineering spaces. All-in, the *Voltaic* represented a four-hundred-twenty-million-dollar investment.

We enjoyed the first course of delicious crab bisque and a salad of fresh greens. Then as promised, large lobsters, perched atop artfully prepared plates, paraded out, two at a time, carried by the graceful team of servers.

As we ate, Carl asked, "Michael, is your contract with Mexico lucrative for you?"

"That's a little forward, there, Carl. But yes, I am satisfied with the terms of our agreement."

"Forgive me. I tend to be a little direct. My world moves too fast at times."

"Not a problem," I said

"Through a subcontractor relationship, my company is working for a contingent of the Mexican government as well."

"Is that so? Like Goddard Petroleum, perhaps? Are you at liberty to discuss it?"

Carl raised his glass to me. "Yes, the little flyover was unnecessary showboating. My client is a Texan after all. But no, unfortunately, it would be a little premature to discuss details, except to say, some developments in our project have surfaced in which I think you and your team could play an important role."

"Our dance card is pretty full right now. What'd you have in mind?"

"In the process of completing our project, we discovered valuable resources wholly unrelated to our originally contracted work and unknown by our client or the Mexican government. Once recovered, these resources represent a significant upside bonus for my company. I think some of that upside could be shared with Water Horse Expeditions."

I was starting to regret mentioning the lithium to Secretary Vega, but I had taken the chance in order to stir the pot. Now we'd just have to see what ingredients came to a boil first.

"Mr. Fayhee, it's my experience that no one rides for free. What would you require of my team to share in this upside?"

"With the use of your crew and vessel, our recovery operations could move more swiftly. But at the very minimum, it would simply require your silence."

Morgan subtly placed his fork back on the table and put his hand in his lap, raising his napkin to wipe his mouth. Morgan's movement caused Sims to stiffen noticeably in his chair.

"Mr. Fayhee, unless the number of Marlin and Mahi we counted while conducting our survey has become a deep, dark state secret, my silence seems a little irrelevant."

Fayhee smiled broadly. "Michael, I invest a ridiculous amount of money to ensure that there's very little that happens on the surface—or beneath—this expanse of water between the US and Mexico that I don't know about."

"Well, Carl, perhaps the Mexican government should have contracted Fayhee and the *Voltaic* to count fish."

The smile disappeared from the man's face and he placed both hands flat on the table as he made intense eye contact. "Or perhaps you should make smarter business decisions for you and your organization."

My grip on the rocks glass tightened. Then as I looked across the table at the man with his black-rimmed glasses and skinny build, I saw what he really was. Carl Fayhee, although brilliant, was a boy that had bought his power and influence with wealth and now wanted to use it to bend the world to his whim, without regard to consequence. The word asshat popped into my mind and I almost laughed, but instead I took a healthy sip of Carl's expensive scotch.

Morgan, sensing dinner was over, pulled his cell phone from his pocket and dialed Beau for our ride back.

Setting my glass back on the table, I met Fayhee's menacing stare with a friendly smile. "Aehh, Carl, I always make the effort to listen to advice from men clearly as smart and successful as yourself. But unfortunately the word 'smart' . . . and my judgment, rarely collide."

Morgan and I stood along with Sims quickly following suit. Carl Fayhee sat stoically and continued his meal.

With as friendly a voice as I could muster, I said, "Mr. Fayhee, thank you for the drinks and dinner. You have a beautiful and remarkable vessel."

Fayhee raised his glass without making eye contact. "Best of luck to you, Brothers Gannon," he said and nonchalantly continued his meal.

We walked aft, through the salon, past the stares of three over-pumped crewmen, and out onto the expansive aft deck with Sims hulking shadow trailing close behind. After closing the aft salon doors, Sims reached and took hold of Morgan's arm, stopping him. "MG, listen. This operation could change everything for a couple of guys like us. The Mexican officials are getting what they wanted, Goddard Petroleum's getting what they paid for, and we get a bonus. Everyone wins and it benefits America, to boot. It's found money, man."

Morgan looked down at where Sims held his arm, and Sims released him. "Sims, this isn't a side hustle in the desert. Governments and billionaires are involved here. And I suspect that the fisherman and his dog and a boat full of sport divers were just collateral damage."

Sims looked down at his feet and remained silent for a few seconds before saying, "Fayhee's in too deep to stop now, MG. He'll finish what he started. He's hard-wired that way and he has unlimited resources to do it. If you don't want in, maybe you and Michael could run to the Keys for Christmas. I'm sure Fayhee would cover any losses from your contract."

Morgan shook his head and looked at the man who would not meet his eyes. "Sims. How long have we known each other? Does that sound like me?"

Sims hung his head with a subtle shake.

"You're a good man, Sims. The work you and I did together on the Teams saved a lot of lives and kept people at home safe. Don't let a small taste of a billionaire's pie change that for you."

Sims silently stared out into the open Gulf. The sound of Beau approaching in the RIB broke the moment. I stepped forward and extended my hand. "Thanks again for the invite, Sims. It was nice to see you."

He shook my hand, but didn't reply as Beau pulled the

RIB against the massive stern of the superyacht, and Morgan and I stepped into our water taxi.

A boyish grin flashed on Sims's face as he added, "Morgan, did I mention it's an insane amount of money?"

With genuine affection, Morgan smiled back at his old friend. "It always is, brother. It always is."

Without another word, Beau leaned on the throttles and the big outboards growled, as the counter-rotating props clawed at the water, punctuating the end of a foreboding dinner.

Chapter 16

WE RAN TWO MILES from the *Voltaic* before I stepped back to the storage box and lifted the lid. Jas lay in the box, knees up, hair still soaking wet, sipping a bottled water.

"Hey, boss. How was dinner?"

My shoulders relaxed, seeing her safe, and I extended my hand to help her out of the locker. When we rejoined Morgan and Beau behind the helm console, I asked, "Anything?"

"Plenty," Jas replied.

"You only thought that boat was big above the waterline. She's got even more going on below the surface," Beau said.

"They're definitely doing something to the bottom below the boat," Jas added. "I'll pull the images and footage as soon as we get back."

Morgan stood holding a side rail to the console hardtop and stared straight ahead as we sped, skimming across the top of the calm, dark water headed for home. As different as Morgan and I were from one another, the rumored twin mental connection was a real thing. So as much as I wished I didn't know what he was thinking, Morgan spoke and confirmed it. "They'll come before dawn. We'll need to be ready."

"I was afraid you'd say that," I replied.

"That doesn't sound good," Beau said.

"I think we know who's behind most of the trouble here in the Gulf," I said.

"Did Fayhee admit to anything?" Jas asked.

"He certainly admitted to wanting our silence," Morgan said.

"Our silence? What did he want us to do?" Jas asked.

"Well, they tried to make an offer we couldn't refuse," I said.

"But let me guess, you refused," Jas said.

I shrugged my shoulders, and we all rode quietly for the last few minutes of the ride. Goddard and Fayhee were taking what didn't belong to them. And they'd keep on taking it and hurting anyone that got in the way until they took it all, or until someone stopped them. We could take the evidence we'd discovered and go straight to Mateo's superiors at

CISEN. Then point our bow northeast and run for the Keys. The Mexican government had the resources to handle this. Of course factions within the Mexican government were behind part of it. How many more innocent people would be hurt as the power brokers played natural resource chess in the Gulf? As I recalled the smug and dismissive manners of Carl Fayhee at the end of our evening, my pulse began to drum in my ears and my jaw clenched. And I could sense it in Morgan as well. He could see a Sims-sized train wreck coming and we'd have to decide how close to the tracks we wanted to stand when it came. But in true Gannon fashion, we both hated the cheap seats.

As Beau brought the RIB up to the stern of the *Water Horse*, Rudy already had the lifting harness lowered near the water. Harper stood with his front paws on the stern rail, barking his welcome. Morgan and I hooked in the lifting harness, and I called Rudy on the radio. "Lift away." And within seconds, the slack in the cables became taunt, and we lifted free of the water. On the controls of the crane, Rudy expertly lifted us up and over the rail, across the deck, and we gently kissed down into the RIB's cradle. Our movement had barely stopped before Harper leapt over, clearing the port side tube, landing in the cockpit. He welcomed us all back aboard, rubbing his oversized head against thighs and licking hands.

"Best welcome home I've had in a while," Beau said.

"If you stopped shoving people into storage boxes, you may get better results," Jas said.

"Hey! . . . I—"

"Stop," Morgan said. "You'll only encourage her."

Ten minutes later, the entire crew sat in the edit bay staring at the large monitors that displayed a slideshow of images and videos captured below the *Voltaic*. A window within the frame showed Ellie on a videoconference link. Jas had linked her in for the show and tell. She sat at her computer with a blanket around her shoulders and a big box of tissues in front of her on her desk. Her nose and eyes were red, but she sat up straight and put on a strong face.

"How ya feeling, sis?" Morgan asked.

"I got slimed, but I'm handling it," she said, sounding like she had a clothespin on her nose.

"El, are you seeing these images okay?" Jas asked.

"Yeah, but I'm still not believing what I'm seeing."

We all sat speechless as the night vision pictures cycled one after another. The images captured from the underside of the superyacht looked like something out of a Bond film. A mass of hoses descended from a compartment opening in the bottom of the immense hull. Many of the hoses led into the top of a box-type device twelve feet below the hull. The hoses exited the boxes, continuing down and into holes in the bottom, thirty feet below.

"Those hoses look like they'd fit this," Rudy said. And as I turned to face him, he tossed me the metal ring I'd left on his workbench earlier. I caught it and gave it a few turns while looking at the images on the screens, then set it on the desk.

"Dredging hose," I said.

"Dredging! Dredging what?" Ellie asked.

I stood, watching the looping images repeat, and the pieces of my crazy theory I had after our first dive, all fell into place. Then after our cryptic dinner conversation aboard the *Voltaic*, I knew there was no doubt. "Goddard's paying them to dredge the islands into the limestone caverns below," I said.

"Ingenioso," Mateo muttered quietly. "What do you think they used the metal rail we found in the first cavern for?" he asked.

"I think they used it as a rail system to pull lengths of hose deeper into the cavern to give them more space to pump the sand from the atoll," I said.

"So they're dredging the sand from the island directly into the caverns below the island?" Ellie asked.

"Could be," Rudy said. "It'd be easy to hide pumps big enough to dredge this sand inside that big of a hull."

"What better place to hide an island, other than right under where it was," Jas said. "There's no barges or other ships needed."

"Right," Morgan said. "They pull up to an atoll, dredge it into the cavern below, pull anchor, and leave."

Other hoses extending from the opening in *Voltaic*'s bottom led to large cylinders suspended halfway between the bottom of the boat's hull and the sandy floor of the Gulf. These cylinders also had hoses that exited from their lower end.

"Any ideas on the large cylinders?" Mateo asked.

"I think they just stumbled on the lithium in the process of dredging the islands away. I suspect there's some type of filtering mechanism inside the cylinders," I answered.

"Mateo is right, it's genius. Even if Goddard was on board to see the operation, he probably wouldn't know anything was up," Beau said.

Morgan added, "And the entire operation happens under water. Anyone in the area or passing satellites just sees a big pleasure yacht. By the time anyone really notices one of the small atolls is missing, everyone is gone and Mexico loses another territorial tentacle into the Gulf, along with a little more of their oil exploration rights."

"Fayhee gets paid by Goddard, who's paying off someone in the Mexican government to look the other way. Then Fayhee sells the lithium in an inflated market, getting paid twice," I finished.

"He has so many fringe energy deals going, he could sell the lithium and no one would suspect it came from this operation," Ellie said over the video chat.

Rudy, who stood leaning against the hatch frame with Harper at his side, snapped, "Yeah, well, it might be pretty clever, but innocent people are getting killed."

"Secretary Vega is part of this," Mateo said.

"She sure seemed anxious to brief other colleagues when she rushed off," I said.

"I've already called CISEN and arranged for increased surveillance on Vega's phone and data taps."

Jerry Styles, who'd been quiet the whole time, piped up. "This all seems like a double-double cross. Fayhee is cheating Goddard, who is cheating the government, and now maybe Vega feels like she's being cheated out of the lithium. Kind of begs the question, who shows up shooting first—a covert team from Secretary Vega's people, the Mexican Navy, or team *Voltaic*?"

Morgan said, "It'll be option three. The *Voltaic* boys will show up first. If they can eliminate us from the equation, along with any proof of the lithium extraction operation, they have a chance of bluffing their way through the rest."

"El, we're uploading these images to you now. Can you

do some additional digging on Secretary Vega? It seems like there's enough here to expose Fayhee and Goddard, at least."

"Two more Advil and I'm on it," she said.

"We'll ring you back first thing in the morning with an update."

Subtly, I gave Jas a sign to cut the video conference feed. "Hey, Michael—"

And the connection ended.

"You'll pay for that." Jas laughed.

"I don't think I want our baby sister to hear this next part."

"I assume they'll come hard?" Beau asked.

"I'm not sure Sims knows any other way," Morgan said.

More innocent people were probably going to be hurt as this unraveled and I knew what I wanted to do. But there were other people I had to think about here, and I cared deeply for all of them. "We can pull the hook and make for the Keys right now."

After a brief silence, the group erupted in protest. Beau stood and quieted the group. "I don't want to speak for everyone, but I don't want to go anywhere. We have the advantage. We know they're coming and this is our home."

Shouts of agreement roared from the group and I felt flattered that Beau felt that way about the boat. Morgan let the commotion settle and said, "Guys, this isn't a bar fight.

These boys will come hard. They've been babysitting millionaires for months. The men are bored, pumped up, and they'll be itching for a fight."

"They'll underestimate us for sure," Jas said.

"Maybe," said Morgan. "But it won't change how hard they'll hit us."

Rudy took a step forward. "Boys, I've experienced being boarded before. I swore if it ever happened again, I would fight like hell's fury itself, never giving up. So put me in the RIB, cause I'm stayin'."

"Well, it has to be unanimous," I said.

Around the cabin, all hands shot in the air. I looked at Dr. Cruz. "Mateo?"

He nodded confidently.

Morgan stood next to me and scanned the group, making eye contact with each individual, and with an assuring nod, said, "Let's get ready."

Chapter 17

OVER THE NEXT NINETY MINUTES, each team member rotated, being outfitted from Morgan's den of trouble. We weren't looking for this fight. We certainly didn't want it. But if Sims's team from *Voltaic* intended to board our boat, our home, and threaten our livelihood, we would defend it with everything we had. And what we had was considerable. Everyone received sidearms, throat mic coms, and bullet resistant vests. Beau and I also carried our Mossberg shotguns with large shot rounds. Morgan carried one of the compact HK416 rifles and issued one to Jerry Styles as well. I made the decision to assign Jerry to the pilothouse roof on overwatch. He would also help coordinate our movements on our discreet coms as we positioned ourselves around the ship to best confront any hostiles who attempted to board us. Jerry was a great shot with a rifle, but the least physical member of the crew. He sparred with us regularly, but the rest of the team was much more effective in close combat skills. Jerry would step in front of a moving train for any of us, but his knack of looking at fast moving situations and slowing them down into effective action was his biggest asset. Then last to kit up was Rudy.

"No, I'm good. I keep everything I'd need with me in the shop."

Morgan looked at me, and I shrugged.

"Are you sure, Rudy?" Morgan asked.

"Oh, I'm sure. I will take one of the vests though. Not that it does anything for your melon."

Morgan pulled another vest from the rack. "Here, try this," Morgan said as he handed Rudy a vest. "You need any help fitting it?"

Rudy rolled his eyes and snapped the vest out of Morgan's hand. "I'll be in the shop."

Just before four a.m., we were as ready as we were going to be. The decks and most of the boat lay dark, except for a few cabin and galley lights. I knew it wouldn't fool anyone, but giving the appearance that we all just hit the rack for the evening was the best idea I had. Sims would know better, but maybe the other thick-skulled boys would let their guard down just enough to make a difference.

At ten minutes after four, Jerry's voice came over my coms. "I've got something heading this way. Low on the water. Too far out for specifics . . . standby."

Jerry was using a night vision scope that was good out to about five miles, but there'd be too much noise and grain in the optics for any detail until the target was closer. "Roger that," I replied.

Morgan and I had positioned ourselves on the bow behind the anchor windlass. Morgan looked at his watch. "Well, he's still predictable."

"I keep hoping you'll be wrong about one of these situations," I said.

"You and me both," he answered. "Did you make that call?"

I nodded. "The petty officer spun up some boats, but this will all be over before they arrive. No choppers available."

"Good to know government bureaucracy is a global problem," said Morgan.

My earpiece squawked. "I gotta RIB. Three miles out. Looks like a seven-man team." The call came as no surprise, but the confirmed reality landed with a heavier weight than I'd expected.

Morgan keyed his throat mic. "Okay guys, remember our

brief. They'll split their team. Two will throw a hook or come up the anchor chain on the bow, and four will go to the stern. With seven, they'll leave a man in the boat to recover them."

"Roger that," Beau responded. He and Jas took positions behind tall lockers on the aft work deck.

"Rudy, you good?" I called.

"We're good, Captain."

"One mile out," Jerry called.

It was very tempting to have Jerry open up on them before they could arrive. Logic said they were coming with lethal harm in mind. But until they tried to board us, we were civilians in Mexican waters, not a war zone. Fifty years in a Mexican prison was not the way we wanted this to go.

"Fifty yards," whispered Jerry.

The faint purr of an outboard motor coming down off plane was a muscle tightening signal that the dance was about to begin.

"Jerry, Morgan and I have the bow, rotate and cover the guys on the stern."

"Will do."

The quiet bubbling outboard held steady on the bow for fifteen seconds and then began ghosting quietly down the port side. My heart thumped against the tight fit of the bullet resistant vest. Morgan's training took over and I took control of my breathing and my heart rate slowed. No grappling hooks appeared on the rail, so it seemed the individuals assigned to board from the bow had opted for the anchor chain approach. I visualized the men ascending hand over hand up the large anchor chain. I counted slowly to ten, then keyed my mic and whispered. "Rudy, light us up."

The suddenness of every deck light and new underwater lights powering up in a single instant had the intensity of a strange explosion without the boom, then the entire ship-wide speaker system blared the edgy guitar intro to AC/DC's "Back in Black." I loved me some Rudy.

The first over-muscled man swung a leg over the gunnel on the bow. And as he stood from his squatted position, I stood up from behind the windlass and lunged forward, cracking the man with a smashing jab to the chin with the butt of my Mossberg. He crumpled on the deck as his partner came over the rail. The second man was more prepared with his weapon raised as he cleared the bow. He fired a shot that whizzed by my left ear, and Morgan fired twice, striking the man in the chest. The man wore a vest, but at this range, if the massive impact of the 45mm NATO round wasn't fatal, he would probably wish it was. He fell beside his companion. I flex-cuffed the first man, removed his Glock 9mm from his holster, and tucked it into my vest.

Jerry's voice came over our coms. "The other men are at the stern."

Morgan checked the second man's pulse and looked at me. "Flex-cuff him as well."

As I bound the second man's hands, Morgan picked up the man's weapon off the deck and tucked it into his vest.

Over the thunderous refrains of Angus and Brian Johnson proclaiming, "Yes, I'm back in black," the booming report of a shotgun cut through the music. Morgan and I broke and ran aft down the side deck. Halfway down the port side, the sharp crack of two rapid handgun rounds proceeded another shotgun BOOM, echoing through the cool predawn. We arrived on the aft deck three seconds later, weapons raised to find a bona fide Mexican standoff.

Beau and Mateo stood weapons up, aiming at two men. One of them, Sims. He spun, pointing his handgun in our direction and his other hand raised in the air.

"Whoa, whoa, everybody, let's just slow this down a little," Sims called.

Sims had two men down; one appeared dead near the stern rail and the other lay hit but alive, for now. Harper stood over the prone figure with his jaws locked firmly across his throat, his deep menacing growl serving as a constant reminder for the man to remain still.

Morgan and I kept our weapons shouldered and pointed directly at Sims. I looked to my left, and Rudy was sitting down on the deck halfway out the aft cabin hatch. His upper left shoulder had taken a hit. He was losing blood, but was conscious and pissed.

"Damn jack-wagons, come on our boat. Come on!"

"MG, this is just business. It's just so much money, let's you and I just fix it."

"You seem a little outgunned at the moment, big man," Morgan said.

"There's a C-4 charge stuck to the waterline on the transom and Bobby out there in the RIB has the remote, so let's not get all caught up in the force count."

A quick glance fifty yards off the stern verified the presence of another over-pumped man at the helm of their RIB with his hand raised in the air, holding a small black box. I couldn't hit him from here with the shotgun and it was just as likely he'd contract if I hit him and squeeze the detonator button anyway.

I keyed my mic. "Jerry, Rudy's hit. Kill the music and grab the med kit on your way down."

"On my way."

"Look," said Sims, "I just need the soil samples and we'll need to trash any computers. You can pull the anchor, turn northeast and be sitting at Sloppy Joe's in Key West in a day's run. We'll get paid by Goddard. We'll sell our other product, and no one will be the wiser."

"Or what?" Morgan said calmly.

"Bobby pushes the button. You have a three-foot hole in your transom, letting the Gulf erase the evidence. And we get paid anyway."

The music stopped, making it easier to concentrate as Jerry appeared through one of the aft cabin hatches, rushing to help Rudy. He cut away Rudy's vest to gain access to his shoulder wound. "He's losing a good bit of blood, Captain."

I glanced at Rudy but kept my rifle pointed at Sims's chest. "Do everything you can, Jerry."

"I think we can fix this, Sims. You and I can settle it right now," Morgan said.

"How's that work?" Sims asked.

Morgan lowered his rifle and propped it against the cabin. "If you win, you smash and take what you need and let us limp home. If I win, you go back to Fayhee, and tell him you destroyed the computers and the samples."

"Shit, man, he'll never buy that."

"If you win, you won't have to sell it."

Sims smiled and lowered his handgun. "So I take your stuff, trash your computers, *and* I beat you half to death. You sure you want to ride that ride, old buddy?"

"All these years, I've never seen anyone beat you. It does make a guy wonder."

Sims tossed his handgun to the last man on his team that was still standing. Then Morgan and Sims took a few cautious steps toward one another in the center of the work deck.

Sims's smile, along with any air of lightness, drained from his face and was replaced by the dead-eyed stare of a shark. The two men made a half circle around one another as they began setting their stances. "Let's get this done," Sims snarled.

I lowered the shotgun and Sims's man lowered his weapon, followed by Mateo and Beau. Morgan struck Sims with a series of kicks and punches that he deflected easily. Sims threw an openhanded grab with his considerable reach, getting a handhold on Morgan's vest. But Morgan spun clear and countered over the top, landing a lightning quick right hook to Sims's face, snapping the giant's head to the side with an audible crack. Morgan quickly hop-stepped back out of range. Sims shook his big head and spit, wiping the blood from his lip. His expressionless eyes caught Morgan's, and he motioned with his right hand. "Come on."

I turned my head, keyed my mic, and whispered, "Where's Jas?"

Beau met my glance and jerked his head in the direction of over the side.

Over the side?

Morgan's punches and kicks bounced off Sims with little effect. Sims sprang forward, launching a massive front kick with a leg that looked like a battering ram. The kick struck Morgan in the chest, expelling all the air from his body and launching him backward six feet, depositing him onto his back on the deck. Morgan rolled to his knees and stood stooped, bent over with his hands on his knees, trying to re-place some of the oxygen kicked out of his lungs. I couldn't see how Morgan would ever inflict any real damage to this freak of nature. Sims just tilted his mini-fridge-sized head, stretching his neck to one side, firing off the sound of cas-cading cracks in the vertebrae in his neck. He was just getting warmed up.

To my surprise, Morgan sprang back at Sims again. The giant's angle of attack was just so much higher. He blocked Morgan's quick punches with his massive forearms, then came around with a quick downward cross, catching Morgan across the chin, snapping his head to one side and collapsing him to one knee. Sims spun into a roundhouse kick and con-nected with the left side of Morgan's head and sent him skidding across the deck and rolling near Sims's remaining teammate. The man raised his foot and knee to add more punishment to Morgan as he struggled to get back to his feet.

"Eh, eh. I wouldn't do that if I were you." Beau had taken two quick steps closer to the man and had his Mossberg lev-eled and aimed for a shot that would remove the man's whole head. "Just back up there, Mr. Thick Neck."

"Morgan?" I called.

"No," Morgan answered, as he got back to his feet. He had a cut above his left eye, and it had already started to swell. Morgan now raised his right hand and motioned to Sims. "Come on."

Sims charged at Morgan with his dead-shark eyes, unleashing a combo of punches that would cripple anyone. Morgan ducked them both and countered with two fast shots to Sims's kidneys, but the big man came around with an elbow as Morgan raised his head and it connected with Morgan's jaw, sending Morgan to his knees on the deck for a second time. And this time, he seemed barely conscious with his head hanging as he struggled to pull things together. He couldn't take much more of this. No man could. There's no way I was going to stand here and let Sims beat my brother half to death. I was going to have to make a decision quickly. We could shoot Sims and his man, but we'd just be blown up by the man with his finger on the trigger to the C-4 charge. Or Beau and I could both fire on Buddy out in the RIB and hope for the best. Neither option seemed very good. And where in the hell was Jas?

Sims approached Morgan and interlaced the fingers on both of his massive hands, raising them to deliver a crippling downward blow to my kneeling brother. Suddenly, Morgan's head snapped up as he swung from the ground, plowing an upward right directly into Sims's crotch, doubling him over. As Sims spewed out a guttural grunt and exhalation of air, Morgan exploded up off the deck, striking Sims under the chin with his right knee. The big man's nose made a sickening crunch, and he swiveled backward, landing hard on his back with a thunderous impact that sounded like a large livestock animal collapsing to the ground.

On unsteady feet, Morgan turned toward me, taking a few steps, and I did the same, rushing to help support him.

"Morgan!" Beau yelled.

BOOM.

Chapter 18

MY HEART HUNG IN MY CHEST. I locked eyes with Morgan and saw both our worst fear reflected back in his eyes. I didn't feel any pain, so the bullet had to have hit Morgan. My eyes tore over my brother's body, scanning for an exit wound as he took his last stumbling step into my arms. "Where are you hit?"

"It's not me, are you hit?" he gasped. I shook my head.

We turned together to see what happened. Sims sat on the deck, arm extended, holding a pistol. His pant leg pulled up to reveal an empty ankle holster. His eyes focused on the bullet hole in the head of his own man, who lay face down, motionless on the steel deck in a pool of his own blood.

"Captain," Beau gasped. "The guy raised his gun to shoot, and before I could get off a shot, Sims shot him."

Sims dropped his arm and stared at the deck between his legs.

"Hey, Captain!"

We all looked up over the stern to find Jas, dripping wet, standing in the cockpit of *Voltaic*'s RIB, holding her Sig 9mm firmly against the back of Buddy's meaty skull.

"You got any more of those flex-cuffs?"

In her free hand, she held the charge detonator. She aggressively pushed the barrel of the handgun forward on the man's skull and snarled a command at him I couldn't hear. Buddy engaged the boat's transmission and motored slowly toward the boarding platform on *Water Horse*. Beau kept his shotgun trained on Sims as he rolled to one knee, reholstered his backup revolver, and raised both hands in the air.

I tossed a pair of flex-cuffs to Mateo as he rushed to meet Jas and the tender as it approached the stern. Sims carefully got to his feet and Morgan gave Beau the sign that he could lower his weapon.

On the southern horizon, I could see blue lights flashing in the predawn light, signaling the approach of Petty Officer Morales's patrol boats. Sims and Morgan stood and looked at each other for several long moments before Sims said, "I guess we still don't know, MG."

"I guess not."

Jas came up the steps from the boarding platform, the detonator in one hand and a dripping magnetic C-4 charge in the other. Mateo remained on the boarding platform, covering the flex-cuffed man in the RIB. Sims turned toward the boarding ladder and Beau took a step forward, raising the shotgun at him. Morgan raised his hand. "Let him go, Beau."

Reluctantly, he lowered the Mossberg. Sims proceeded down the boarding ladder and stepped over into the RIB. "Mateo, let 'em go," Morgan said. And Mateo lowered his handgun.

Sims pulled out a folding knife, cut Buddy's cuffs, and motioned for him to take off. Seconds later, the RIB roared out of sight to the east, back in the direction of the *Voltaic*.

I rushed to Rudy, who was sitting with his back against the frame of the hatch. Jerry seemed to have the bleeding under control, but Rudy was clearly woozy from the blood loss. The bullet had hit him in the shoulder strap of his vest, but above the armor plating. Now that the vest was cut away, we could see there was no exit wound. So at the very least, he would need surgery to remove the bullet. "How you doin', Rudy?"

"I won't lie, Cap. It hurts like hell." He looked across the deck, a little groggy-eyed. "Harper! You can let him go." The low growl stopped, and Harper released his grip on the man's throat. Harper's former prisoner appeared to still be conscious, but he elected to remain laying right where the beast had released him. Harper charged over to Rudy and gave him a series of licks on the cheek.

"I'm good, boy, I'm good. We kept them jack-wagons from taking the boat, didn't we?"

I put my hand on Rudy's good shoulder. "You did just that, Rudy. No unfriendly boards this boat without a fight."

I stood and stepped over to Morgan. "You okay?"

"I'll be sore as hell for a few days, but yeah, I'm fine. I assume this is our petty officer friend approaching?"

"A little late, but yes. And even though it's over, reinforcements arriving feels good."

Morgan smiled. "Yeah, I might need another minute before I go another round with anyone."

"Well, you do look like hell."

"I'm good enough to go with you right now," he said. We both laughed.

The patrol boats were almost on us, and Beau and Jas prepared lines and fenders to receive the three vessels alongside. When the boats were secured, Petty Officer Morales was first aboard and I met him with a handshake. He looked around the deck and then back at me. "Looks like you've had a busy morning, Captain."

"I've got a man with a gunshot wound that needs attention. Any way we can get a chopper out here?"

The petty officer yelled a series of commands to crew members still on the patrol boat, and after a quick back-and-forth exchange in Spanish, he turned back to me. "A medical chopper is on the way. And I have a medic in our crew that can assist. Now, can you tell me what occurred here this morning?"

"A RIB with a crew of seven armed men approached from the east and attempted to board our vessel, and we defended ourselves."

"And a crew of a marine research vessel repelled these armed men"—he waved his arms across the deck as his men worked to collect the five *Voltaic* men on four stretchers and one body bag—"and left all this?"

"This is our home, Petty Officer Morales. So, yes, the crew of this marine research vessel, did all this."

The thunderous boom from the explosion stopped everyone on the boat where they stood. We all rushed to the starboard side of the boat as a massive fireball rose over the eastern horizon several hundred feet high. We all stood, watching in shock. I looked at Morales and said, "The *Voltaic*."

Morales shouted commands at his crew and eight of his men scrambled and boarding one of the three patrol boats, leaving the remaining men and boats finishing the cleanup aboard *Water Horse*. Heading for his boat, the petty officer looked back at me and shouted, "Captain! Are you coming?"

Morgan and Mateo sprang into action, beating me as they rushed aboard the patrol boat. Already moving, I turned to Jerry and Jas. "Get Rudy on that chopper."

"We've got him, Michael, go," said Jas.

I stepped over onto the vessel's side deck, barely finding a handhold before the boat pilot slammed the throttles to the stops, pointing the boat toward the towering cloud of flame and smoke. We tore across the calm morning waters as the sun climbed above the horizon. The smoke cloud continued to billow skyward into the early morning light as I turned to Morgan. "Thoughts?"

"If someone made an attempt to take the boat, they were probably surprised and under-manned, because seven of their crew members were all over here, trying to ruin our day."

Fifteen minutes later, we approached a surreal scene. The beautiful, gleaming behemoth of modern marine design, the *Voltaic,* was a smoldering hulk, with most of the boat gone above the first deck, closest to the waterline. Thick black smoke billowed from every foot of what was left, and burning debris covered the surface of the water for hundreds of yards in every direction.

Mateo looked out at the destruction and turned to me. "Vega is covering her tracks."

"Could she use government forces?" I asked.

"Sicarios," Mateo answered. "If the payments that Vega and her syndicate accepted were even close to what we suspect, they would have a significant budget to higher skilled men as enforcers."

"Who are the other members of the syndicate?" Morgan asked.

"We only have suspicions of a few cabinet ministers, but no real proof," said Mateo.

"I think we're watching most of that proof sink," I said.

The wreck groaned and creaked as the fire continued to weaken the infrastructure that remained floating. A plume of steam shot skyward as seawater penetrated some section of the engineering spaces where water shouldn't be. Seconds later, the remaining part of the hull listed hard over on its port side and the stern section began sinking. What was left of the *Voltaic* was going down. The pilot of the patrol boat engaged the engines and backed us away from the burning wreck another fifty yards.

Loud cracks and groans sounded along the length of the hull section and then became quiet as the wreckage of the bow slowly rose twenty feet into the air and slipped stern first under the calm waters of the Gulf.

We all watched quietly as the hulk disappeared peacefully beneath the surface, leaving a boiling turbulent mass of bubbles and debris.

A pang of remorse hit me as I thought about all the people on the ship that had just sunk before us. Some innocent, some not. But did it have to come to this? We hadn't assaulted the *Voltaic*, but yet, we were now in the middle of all this. Justified, provoked. Aggressor or defender, every soldier on a battlefield possesses some fraction of the responsibility.

I turned away from the rippling water where a ship had been and suddenly I was knocked forward to my knees on the deck. Everyone braced themselves and spun to see the explosion and water erupt water thirty feet into the air. The upward force of the blast created a six-foot wave that now careened toward the patrol boat, rolling us severely, sending everyone on board grappling for a hold of anything to keep from being thrown overboard. The wave passed, and the boat stabilized on to a now calm ocean surface, that was eerily quiet.

"Everyone okay?" Morales called out.

Head nods and affirmatives came from the group.

"What do you think caused that?" Mateo asked.

"Maybe something from the experimental propulsion system," I replied as a guess.

"There," shouted Morgan, pointing twenty yards away off the stern.

We all turned to see where Morgan was pointing. The pilot engaged the transmission and maneuvered us in that direction. As the boat got closer, we could see it was a body floating face down. Ten yards closer, I could now see what Morgan knew all along. It was a beast of a man with singed clothes. The boat pulled alongside the body and Morgan reached over the gunnel and I joined him as we struggled to heft the oversized body into the boat. Sims's head and chest were badly injured by impact trauma. Morgan and I carefully laid him on the deck, and the petty officer brought a white drop cloth from a body recovery kit he retrieved from the bow. He handed me the drape. I paused a moment, looking down at Sims. I was filled with a strange feeling of conflict. He came fully prepared to harm us and destroy our home. But his actions in the last seconds of our fight gave me a glimpse of who he was. The kind of man that allowed himself to be buried under the grime of wanting. I began covering Sims's lower body and Morgan took over as he gave his former teammate a long last look before he reverently pulled the drape over Sims's face.

"Did you know this man?" the petty officer asked.

"Yes, a long time ago, I did," Morgan answered.

The VHF radio on the helm exploded to life with rapid fire Spanish. "Secure yourselves," Morales shouted, as the helmsman slammed the throttles forward and the patrol boat's twin engines' deep roar increased and the vessel surged, pointing back to the west. Mateo's face grew grim, and I shouted at him over the roar of the engines. "What were they saying on the radio?"

"A group of armed men are attacking the *Water Horse*."

Chapter 19

My adrenaline surged as the scream of the engines' high RPMs pushed past any practical max became deafening. A helicopter with its cabin dipped forward for maximum speed, thumped overhead, away from the *Water Horse*'s position, and I had some small feeling of relief to see that it was a search and rescue medical chopper. I hoped they'd managed to get Rudy off the boat and on his way to medical attention before the attack. Morgan stared straight ahead, the muscles of his jaw flexing as he clinched his teeth. My stomach dropped as I felt sure we were both thinking the same thing. Dammit, we'd left our crew short-handed and outgunned. Jerry's words about a double-double cross screamed through my mind. There was at least one other set of potential aggressors on the field and we'd turn our back to them.

I leaned forward, irrationally trying to will another knot of boat speed from the already over-revved motors. Finally, after an agonizing amount of time that seemed like hours, I could see the outline of *Water Horse* on the horizon, but I couldn't see any activity. Two minutes later, we slowed on the starboard side of *Water Horse* with the smell of cordite still hanging thick in the air. Smoke still rose off the barrels of the fifty-caliber machine guns mounted on the bow of the patrol boats that had fortunately remained behind with the team. The scene was quiet and it was clear that we'd just missed a hell of a scene. My heart raced as I frantically scanned the decks for any sign of our team. Where were they? Morgan checked the mag in his weapon as we got closer to being able to board our boat. Then finally, I exhaled as Beau and Jas appeared around the bow from the port side deck, each still holding HK416 rifles. Jerry stood up from a prone position on the top of the pilothouse with his rifle slung on one shoulder and raised his hand in a relieved greeting.

A quick headcount of our crew added up to the right number, minus Rudy, and I allowed my shoulders to relax a notch. As our pilot maneuvered the patrol boat around the stern of *Water Horse*, we could see the source of the attack.

Fifty yards off the port side of *Water Horse*, two bullet-riddled, flat black military RIBs drifted with two bodies draped over the gunnel of one hull tube. There were no other signs of life aboard either craft. The helmsman positioned us against the *Water Horse* boarding platform and Mateo, Morgan, and I jumped aboard, rushing up onto the stern deck. Beau and Jas met us.

"Is everyone okay?" I asked.

"We're all good, Michael," Beau replied.

"And Rudy," I asked.

"He's stable and the medical chopper is taking him back to Cancun," said Jas. "The flight medic said a surgeon was standing by and Rudy's vitals were as strong as an ox's."

I looked around the deck and back to Jas. "Where's Harper?"

Jas smiled. "We tried to keep him out of the chopper, but he wasn't having it, so the flight medic let him go. I'm sure he's sitting bedside as we speak."

"How'd all this go down?" Morgan asked.

Smiling, our marine was quick to answer. "It seems the enemy drastically underestimated the opposition's force."

My at times overactive motherly instincts in regard to my crew would probably never change, but this team could clearly take care of themselves.

Mateo's sat phone rang, and he stepped away to take the call. Jas turned her face and I could see she had a cut across her cheek, seeping blood. Morgan stood several feet away, quietly talking to Morales. I walked over to one of the dive operation benches and sat heavily, as if someone had pulled my power cord. I stared blankly, watching as Petty Officer Morales's team weapons raised, approached the drifting attack vessels. Other members of Morales's team still rushed around our decks, and the noise of constant radio chatter filled the air with chaos. As I sat, all the noise faded into a dull white static, like watching a movie with the sound turned off. There was so much activity. The men pointing and gesturing. The blood staining our aft deck and the dead men slumped over a hull just off our port side. All this, for oil and lithium? I wondered, in a few hundred years, would we look back at ourselves now like cavemen throwing rocks at one another? Someone sat beside me and leaned against my shoulder, shaking me out of my daze.

"How about you, Michael? You okay?" Jas asked.

I turned to her and smiled. Reaching up, I gently touched the edge of the cut on her cheek. "I will be. I'm much better knowing everyone is okay."

"We are okay, and Rudy's going to be okay."

"Are we crazy for getting involved in these kinds of situations?" I asked.

"What do you mean?"

"Look around, Jas. The deck is covered with spent brass and blood and I just watched a three-hundred-plus-foot yacht sink because it was blown to pieces."

"Michael, do you believe we're doing good?"

I thought about the question. My mind raced through the events of the last thirty-six hours. And even after the litany of near misses and danger, I couldn't escape my answer. "Yes, I do."

"I don't think I ever feel as *alive* as I do when we're working on doing something good," Jas said.

"I feel the same. I always have," I said.

"We all love working on *Water Horse* because you and Morgan lead us. Not because you shelter us from the danger. Look at me, Michael, do I look like someone that needs or wants protecting?" she asked with a slight laugh.

"No . . . No, you don't."

"How about Beau? Morgan? Rudy!? Just keep leading, Michael. Help us keep finding assignments that allow us to do good whenever we can. Many more innocent people would've been hurt if Fayhee and Vega continued to run their operation here."

She placed her hand on top of mine. "Just lead, Captain. We'll follow."

With that, she stood and joined Beau as he worked on securing the deck. Mateo took Jas's place on the bench as he closed the sat phone in his hands.

"I'm assuming that the dead guys out there are Vega's sicarios?"

"It's a sound assumption. With the *Voltaic* and *Water Horse* gone, it would be hard to prove anything. I'm sure they did not expect Petty Officer Morales's team to be here."

"How about the extra surveillance on Vega?"

Mateo paused and looked at his phone. "That's what the last call was. Vega is gone," he said.

"Gone?"

"CISEN raided her office and her home. She is gone. We've already notified Interpol, and they have issued a travel alert for her."

"That leaves most of our proof scattered across the bottom of the Gulf," I said.

"Sí, Captain. But I think we have stopped the damaging activity. Now that we know what was occurring, it will be hard for any bad actors to dredge away our islands. And with some of the information we've discovered about the limestone caverns, perhaps Mexico can become a new resource for lithium production."

"Hopefully, it's a less nasty business than oil exploration," I said.

"I imagine that any resource we view as scarce and valuable will always have its share of unsavory characters."

"Speaking of that, someone will need to diffuse the explosives on this site," I said.

"An explosives unit has already been dispatched. They'll arrive in the next four hours."

"Water Horse can assist in the dive operations for that job," I said.

"That would be very helpful, Michael. I'll let the team leader know."

He paused a moment before saying, "Captain, I know Vega is gone, but we'll find her. And it may take longer to find her co-conspirators, but we will. Together, we accomplished a great deal here. Your team has been invaluable in this operation. My government intends to demonstrate its great appreciation for your work. And I think this region of the Gulf is much safer than it was a few days ago."

I sat and looked out over the beautiful blue water of the shared Gulf of Mexico. It really was a priceless treasure for our two countries. "Well, Doc, I guess we should both just get back to work, yeah?"

"Indeed, Captain. There is much to do."

"After we clear these explosives, are the cerveza and fresh fish still your treat at Marinero Salado?"

Mateo's bigger than life smile beamed. "*Sí, el Capitan.* Until the taps run dry."

Petty Officer Morales's team was wrapping up their duties as the explosives team arrived. I met Morales on the aft deck and he extended his hand. "I think we're done here for now, Captain. We'll need you for a formal debrief in Cancun when you get back in, of course. I think everything is straightforward, but there is an abundance of moving parts here."

"I understand. We will help with the explosives cleanup and head straight for port. I'm really glad you showed up, Eduardo. Thank you."

"We have the calvary down here as well, Michael. If you're ever in the area, I'll always take your call."

"Much appreciated," I said as we shook.

Our team got started with the Explosives Disposal Unit crew by sharing the video and photos we recorded, along with the exact locations of the first charges we found. We also provided dive operations support. They particularly appreciated the use of our ROV, providing live video surveillance, which allowed the team leader to carefully observe each phase of the delicate work. Satisfied they'd located all the hidden devices in the area of Isla Escondida, the explosive disposal team successfully diffused twenty-two deadly charges in all. Left in place, any unwitting investigators or sport divers would have been reduced to fish food and the derelict boats left behind would be explained away by a dozen other circumstances that can happen on the water two hundred miles away from the mainland. It was a pretty thorough tactic to hide any wrongdoing until the players were an ocean away, and beyond suspicion.

At the completion of the six-hour operation, Morgan, Jas, and I treated the EDU team to a simple dinner of Brunswick stew and cold beer from Rudy's stash in the ship's freezer. New friendships were made and it served as a good wind down to the intense day. Mateo insisted on filling in as an extra hand for our trip back to Cancun the next day. My initial doubts about the doctor were now replaced with respect and admiration. He was an honorable man, trying to serve his country the best way he could. The crew even presented him with his own Water Horse Expeditions crew shirt at dinner to the clinking of bottles and cheers.

We were a man down, but Beau would serve as our engineer until we could get Rudy back on his feet. Rudy had already texted him four times this evening with instructions covering everything from filter changes to a reminder that "no one touches my iron skillets." After the fifth text, the marine put his cell phone on silent and set it on top of the galley refrigerator. "He's worse than my mother," he said.

Morgan and Mateo saw our guests to their launch and Jas

and I handled the galley cleanup. I washed and she dried. We joked and laughed a little, talking about nothing of conse- quence. We mostly speculated about how many items we'd have put in the wrong place in the galley. Rudy would be hard to live with his first few days back, even though we both worried about our old salt laying in a hospital twelve hours running from our position. The work wrapped up and the galley grew quiet.

"I am bushed. I'm going to hit the rack," Jas said. "We're anchor up at first light?"

"Yeah, I'm anxious to get back and check on our boys."

"I laugh every time I think of Harper standing guard in the hospital room."

We both laughed.

"I wanted to say thank you," I said. "Thank you for what you said out on deck earlier today. It meant a lot to me."

"I meant it, Michael. We all do." She threw the wadded dishtowel at me, hitting me in the chest. "Now let me hit the rack, you slave driver." And she disappeared through the hatch.

"Good night, Jas," I called.

I fell into my bunk and there was an instant realization of just how wide open we'd been running for the last several days. The fatigue felt like someone pouring a thick, heavy oil down my body from a bucket. I didn't even feel like kicking off my shoes. A knock at the door startled me awake. I rolled out of my bunk and opened my cabin door.

"What you have in the bourbon cabinet?" Morgan asked.

"Ahh, I always have something. Come on in."

"You seemed surprised to see me. You expecting someone else?"

I stepped back and opened the hatch wider for him to enter, walking toward my desk. "Don't you ever sleep?" I asked.

"Sure, whenever I need it."

I opened the bottom cabinet of my desk and reached to grab the bottle closest to the front. It was a bottle of Larceny Barrel Proof. I grabbed two rocks glasses off a small shelf on the bulkhead and poured us both two fingers and handed him his glass.

"Something on your mind, my insomniac twin?" I asked.

Morgan took a sip of the whiskey and held in his mouth before slowly swallowing the warm burn. "I need you to do something with me," he said.

"Name it."

"I asked Petty Officer Morales if he could arrange to release Sims's body to me."

I gave him an odd look as he continued.

"Sims was an only child and his parents have been gone

for a while. He doesn't have any other family. I know he was on the wrong side of this thing, but he was a member of my team and he saved American lives and made a difference when he served." He paused a long moment, then said, "I want to make sure he gets a proper burial."

"Why you?"

"Why not me?"

"Think he would've killed you if that had gone a little different?"

Morgan sat and thought about that through another sip. "I don't know. I do know in the end, he still had my back."

I nodded slowly. "I guess he did."

Chapter 20

The hospital in Cancun was a modern four-story building nestled in a mostly residential area of town. We were due at a debriefing with Mateo and members of the CISEN team in a few hours. We would share the data we'd collected and Mateo's superiors had agreed to let Ellie sit in and share the information she had discovered on the relationship of Goddard Petroleum and Fayhee Energy. But first thing this morning, we needed to check on our friend and engineer Rudy. Morgan and I entered the large double doors and approached the reception desk attended by a very attractive young woman with a welcoming smile and long, dark hair pulled over one shoulder.

"*Buenos días señores. ¿En qué puedo ayudarles?*"

"Good morning, we're here to visit a patient," I said.

Switching seamlessly to English, she said, "What is the patient's name?"

"Rudy Giles," I replied.

"Ohh, señor Rudy! Yes, he is on the second floor, room two fourteen. Mr. Rudy is so sweet," she cooed.

"Thank you, Miss. Have a great day."

"You as well. Please tell Mr. Rudy, Carmen said hola."

"Oh, we will," Morgan said.

Morgan and I walked down the short corridor to the elevator and pushed the up button. The doors opened and we both stepped on. When the doors closed, I said, "He's only been here two days."

"Rudy juju," Morgan replied.

The doors to the second floor opened into a long hallway bustling with activity. We'd have no trouble finding room 214, because there, halfway down the hall on the left side, Harper sat at attention outside one of the patient rooms. We were almost to him, before he turned his big head and spotted us. He did not leave his position, but he panted and banged his big tail against a service cart, announcing our arrival. Before we entered the room, girlish giggling poured from the open door. "Ohh, Mr. Rudy, you are so funny! Can I get you anything else this morning?"

"No, Marisa, just seeing your smile this morning is medicine enough."

"Ahemm," I coughed.

Rudy looked up and saw Morgan and I standing there looking like parents that just caught our teenage son sneaking the car out of the garage. He sat up a little taller.

"Hey, Captain, Morgan. I didn't expect you two until later this afternoon."

"Carmen says, 'ola" Morgan mocked.

I couldn't keep it together and I busted out laughing, Morgan followed suit. Rudy's shoulders eased a little and he gave a crooked smile. "Damn jack-wagon brothers, get in here."

We stepped over to the bed, still laughing. "Michael, Morgan, this is Marisa. She's one of the talented young medical professionals taking care of me."

I extended my hand. "Pleased to meet you. I'm Michael Gannon."

"Morgan. Nice to meet you. Has he been behaving?"

"Oh yes, we've all grown very fond of Mr. Rudy. He has told us many stories and told us all about the two handsome brothers he works with on your beautiful boat, *Water Horse*."

"I bet he has, Marisa," I said.

"And we all love Harper, he is so loyal. He has not left Mr. Rudy's side since he arrived." Then she glanced outside the door and whispered, "The hospital administrator doesn't want him on the floor, but one of us lets Harper up the back steps, as soon as he's gone."

"Hola, Harper." We heard, causing us to turn to the door, as a man we assumed was the doctor entered the room.

"Hey, Doc," Rudy said.

"Good Morning, Rudy. How do you feel this morning?"

"I'm ready to get back to my shop, Doc. I feel fine."

"Good morning, Doctor, I'm Michael Gannon with Water Horse Expeditions. How is our boy, really?"

"Very nice to meet you, Michael. I'm Dr. Ramirez. Mr. Giles was very lucky. We were able to extract the bullet without any permanent damage to the bone or major muscles in his shoulder. The vest material slowed the bullet enough to provide some protection. He will be stiff and sore for several weeks and it may be two months before he regains full range of motion. We will discharge him with a full set of therapy exercises to speed his rehabilitation." He looked at Rudy now. "If our new friend Rudy is diligent, he'll make a complete recovery in a few months."

"Roger that, Doc. I'm on it." Morgan smiled.

Rudy hung his head. "Oh, hell's bells."

"We should be able to discharge Rudy tomorrow morning."

"That is outstanding, Dr. Ramirez," I said.

The sound of alarm bells shattered the light moment, and the foot traffic in the hallway increased dramatically, along with a barrage of Spanish announcements and calls over the hospital PA speakers. Another nurse stuck her head in the door. "Dr. Ramirez, they need you in emergency, right away."

The doctor hurried from the room, and Morgan and I stepped out into the hall. I stopped a young orderly that hurried down the hall in my direction. "What's going on?" I asked.

"There has been an explosion at a government office across town, the injured are being sent here and another hospital."

I looked at Morgan. "Mateo," I said.

Morgan stuck his head back into Rudy's room, where Harper had taken a position at Rudy's bedside. "Rudy, we'll be back to get you both in the morning."

"Hey, wait. What's . . ."

But we were already in a full run for the staircase at the end of the hall because they would be faster. When we reached the sidewalk, I waved down a cab despite the chaos of ambulances and emergency vehicles scrambling in every direction. Jumping in, I said, "Thirty-three Avenue Nader, and there's an extra hundred American, if you can get us there quick."

The cab tore away from the curb and I was already regretting the challenge I had posed to the young driver. The car tilted hard on what felt like two wheels as we cleared the parking lot. Morgan maintained a death grip on the back of the front seat as we ripped through the narrow back streets of Cancun.

"Maybe this isn't related," I yelled over the screaming engine and tire squeals.

"How's our luck ran along those lines so far?" Morgan yelled back.

Up ahead, I could see traffic stopped, and our driver skidded to a stop inches from a car's rear bumper. There were emergency vehicle lights going through cross streets fifty yards further up the crowed street. "This is as far as I can take you," the driver said. I handed him the hundred-dollar bill and we sprang from the cab. We ran down the sidewalk toward the wails of the sirens. At the next cross street, we could see the smoke billowing up over the roofs of the buildings ahead of us.

"Over there!" Morgan pointed two more blocks off to the right. We continued to run. We made the final turn down a small side street, and fifty yards further, the alley opened up on to the next block. We both hard stopped and stared at the scene, as we huffed, completely out of breath. The CISEN offices were on the third floor of the four-story building. All the windows along the street side of the entire structure were blown out. Black smoke roiled out of the openings, chased by orange flames from most of the third floor. There were twenty or more ambulances and emergency vehicles filling the streets and sidewalks. People screamed as they either fled the scene or stood crying on the sidewalk, anxiously waiting to see if friends or loved ones would emerge alive from the burning building. Two fire trucks were simultaneously spraying water into the windows of the burning third floor from raised ladder platforms, as they desperately tried to get the fire under control.

Morgan and I sprinted closer to the building and could now see victims being triaged on the ground in every direction.

We both turned in a circle, trying to take in the enormity of the scene. "I don't even know where to start," Morgan said, still breathing hard.

We made our way carefully through the throng of emergency workers desperately working on injured victims, attempting to stabilize them enough to transport them for care. I stared out across the front courtyard of the building, filled with chaos.

Out of complete chance, I spotted a man on a stretcher being pushed toward an ambulance. The man wore a neon bright golf shirt that stood out even covered with the black of soot and dirt. "I think I found him," I said, as I ran in the man's direction with Morgan right behind me.

It was Mateo. When I reached his side, what I saw caught my breath in my throat. He was badly burned on the left side of his face, neck, and chest. His left eye was sealed shut with burns and swelling. "Hold on," I said to the medic. "He's a friend."

"His condition is very serious, we have to move, now."

I put my hand on the top of Mateo's unburned right hand and his right eye partially opened. His lips moved, but I couldn't hear him.

"Señor, we have to go."

"One second," I barked. I leaned down close to Mateo's face and put my ear near his lips. I listened, then turned my face to meet his eyes and nodded my head. "Go! Go!" I said.

The medics quickly loaded him into the ambulance and Morgan banged twice against the closed rear doors as the rig sped off.

I stood looking up at the burning building, recalling my conversation with Mateo on the *Water Horse* two days before.

"What did he say?" Morgan asked.

He said, "We'll get her."

Chapter 21

Twenty-four hours later, I sat in the passenger seat of a Mexican military vehicle with Petty Officer Morales at the wheel. We wound our way through the rundown neighborhood where the hotel and restaurant workers and tourist boat captains could afford to live as they provided unforgettable holidays to the world's throngs of tourist that flocked to the tropical playground of Cancun. Kids played in abandon lots with half-inflated soccer balls kicked into makeshift goals cobbled together from discarded construction netting and scrap plastic pipe. I rode quietly as Morales wound through the narrow streets, crowded with trash and parked cars, many long since been abandoned. He brought the vehicle to a stop in front of a freshly painted home that showed care and a sense of pride.

"I want to thank you again for your help releasing Sims's body. I know that was a big ask," I said.

"Your brother is trying to give a once honorable man, an honorable burial. For all the problems we have in my country, we've not lost our sense of good and honor."

"Well, I appreciate it Eduardo. It makes me sleep better knowing good men can be found in any bad situation, if we take the time to look."

"Indeed," said Eduardo. "Shall we?"

We exited the car and walked up the neatly swept sidewalk and onto the small stoop. The petty officer knocked on the door. A well put together middle-aged woman opened the door. She wore a casual, yet well-pressed dress and apron. The two exchanged greetings and introductions in Spanish. I was able to cryptically follow before Eduardo thankfully switched to English for my benefit. "Señora García, this is Michael Gimbal."

"Very nice to meet you, señor Gimbal," she said.

"You as well, ma'am. I represent an organization that provides benefits to injured or lost watermen around the world. When we became aware of your son Alejandro's story, his case was elevated to the top of our list. We like to keep the details of our foundation anonymous, but I wanted to personally deliver this to his family."

I handed the envelope to her and she tentatively opened it

just enough to read the amount. Tears filled her large brown eyes and then overflowed down her cheeks.

"Alejandro worked so hard to provide for his sister and I, but I would give everything up to prepare dinner for him one more time. He was a good man, like his father."

"Yes, ma'am, that what we've been told from everyone that knew him. I hope this helps in some small way."

Through tearful quivering lips, she smiled and said, "He is looking down on us and resting better knowing that we have been cared for. Thank you so much, señor Gimbal. Please extend my family's gratitude to your organization."

Eduardo switched back to rapid fire Spanish and Ms. García's face looked surprised as she turned to me.

"You found a home for Alejandro's dog as well?"

"A member of our team developed a bond with him quickly, but if you would like him returned to you, we totally understand."

"He was Alejandro's dog and his alone. He would be lost here with us," she said with a smile.

"If you don't mind me asking. I've been told he is a Scottish deerhound. He seems very out of place in Mexico. Do you know where he came from?"

Ms. García smiled, shaking her head with a small laugh. "A freighter from Europe came into port here. They unloaded, but were forced to leave suddenly to avoid a hurricane that was approaching. In their rush to depart, the poor dog got left behind. Alejandro found him rain soaked sitting on the dock where the freighter was docked. Alejandro brought him home and they've been inseparable for the past three years."

"That sounds about right." I laughed and we all shared a chuckle.

Ms. García thanked me again as we said our goodbyes. Back in the car, Eduardo paused before he started the engine. "I, too, look for good men in the situations I encounter here in my country amid the narcos and now the corruption uncovered with Minister Vega. This time I found that good man in you, Michael. Gracias."

I took out one of my business cards. "You gave me your card and told me you'd always answer. You were true to your word and I'll always be grateful." I handed him my card. "You have my word, I'll always do the same."

Eduardo took the card and looked at it for a beat and placed it in his shirt pocket. "I look forward to the next time our paths cross, Captain." He started the car, and we pulled away from the García home, leaving a tearful mother waving, heartbroken and grateful.

The December sun was bright and warm. We made our arrival on Stock Island, just on the north side of Key West, after a twenty-six-hour run from Cancun. The passage was quiet and somber. It did feel good to be back in the States and even though it was still eight hundred miles further north, it also felt closer to home.

The quirkiness of the Keys was far different from the Low Country of coastal South Carolina, but all coastal communities shared a vibe generated by the water. The poor souls of the Northeast were already in the grip of their first early winter storm, with below zero windchills and a foot of snow. There was no such cold white stuff here. It was eighty-one degrees with a five mile an hour breeze from the east. As I drove north along A1A, the teal-blue of Florida bay filled the half-opened driver's side window, and the darker blue of the Atlantic kept Morgan's attention through his view on the passenger side. He'd been very quiet since our departure this morning at sunup. His US Navy dress-blue jacket hung on a hanger in the back seat of the rental, along with my new sport coat. A bead of sweat was already gliding down the small of my back under my new dress shirt, even though the air conditioning in the small import rental was blowing cold. I knew the "less boat bum" new clothes purchase would be helpful, but I never imagined I'd be pulling at my buttoned collar for extra space so soon, much less, wear them for this kind of occasion so soon. We'd turn northwest in the next few minutes, losing our water view as we entered the desolate part of the drive through the Everglades, leading us north to Homestead and on into Miami, our destination this morning.

"I think you picked a really nice spot," I said, breaking the half hour of silence.

Morgan continued staring out his window at our last glimpses of the Atlantic before he finally said, "He loved warm weather and the tropics. Like you. I remembered this morning about an op we did in the mountains over in the sandbox years ago. He bitched about the cold for three straight weeks. Again . . . like you." He smiled. "But he also loved the fast life of the big city and the super-sized jerk could always make you laugh just before you wanted to poison his canteen. So Miami seemed to fit the bill for both."

"Morales must have pulled a lot of strings to get him released."

"He did, and I think Mateo and the guys at CISEN helped. I owe them both."

"How'd you do with the other arrangements?" I asked.

"A unit from NAS Key West came up yesterday, so they should be all set. Did you get any word on Mateo's condition?"

"He lost his left eye and he'll need several skin graft surgeries for his chest and right arm. It'll be a long road back. Probably a year or more. In a morphine-induced monologue, he mumbled something about his eye patch getting him free cerveza at Marinero Salado."

"I'm sure he'll work the patch." Morgan laughed.

The drive and the silence continued as we entered the endless, undeveloped acers of empty grass and scrub south of Homestead. All this rural empty space stood in such contrast this close to a metro area of six million people.

"This is nice, what you're doing today. Thanks for inviting me to go with you."

"I'm not doing it to be nice. I'm doing it because it should be done. It should be done for his service and what he did in his time on the Teams. But I'm still furious with him. He always had a chip on his shoulder about growing up so poor, I guess he just couldn't shake it."

"Will anyone else be there?" I asked.

"I didn't call anyone. It would just create more questions. After Ellie's story breaks, some of the guys will wonder. A couple of them knew he received an offer to work in Mexico. But no need to assist the speculation. We always knew if something happened to us on a mission, there'd be a chance no one would ever really know what happened."

"You don't think they'd want to pay their respects?"

"If and when they find out, they will, in their own way."

I saw a small gas station coming up on our right and pulled off.

"I'm grabbing a water and hitting the head. Want anything?" I asked.

"I'm good," Morgan said

I grabbed us both waters from the cooler anyway and approached the counter manned by a scruffy bearded man wearing a Caterpillar Diesel hat. An old TV hung crooked on its mount on the wall behind him, running one of the conservative news networks. The sound was down, but the photo displayed on the screen was easy to recognize even through the fuzzy picture of the beat up set. It was Vega with a graphic banner scrolling across the bottom of the screen. "Mexico Energy Secretary flees country amid investigation." From what I could gather through the text on the screen, there weren't many details so far. I stared at the old television, hoping for more information, and the man snapped me out of my daze. "Need anything else?"

"Sorry, just haven't seen the news in a while."

"Trust me, you haven't missed a thing. Just different people that ought to know better, still acting stupid. You know, beauty is skin deep. But stupid . . . goes all the way to the bone."

We both laughed, and I paid the man for the waters.

Back in the car, I tossed Morgan a water, and we got back on the road. "I just caught a blurb on the national news, and they're reporting that Vega has fled the country because of the investigation."

"The fact that she's still out there is not good for us," he said, looking straight ahead. "We may hold some of the only real compelling evidence against her. CISEN lost a lot of data in the attack."

"You think she'd come into the US for us?"

"I'm not sure what she's capable of, and I don't like that."

The small divided two lane road leading us north got bigger and busier with every mile. Within a few minutes, the roads transformed into jammed lanes of congestion and red-light-infested craziness that fill most US metros today. The palm trees and brightly colored buildings helped Miami pull it off with a little more style than most of its northern rivals, but was still just automobile-powered madness. We pulled into the small cemetery that was only a block from Biscayne Bay. The grounds were beautiful, with mature live oaks and the broad sprawling canopies of mature Banyan trees providing large pools of shade across the men and women laid to rest here. The azure water of the bay was so close, and as we stepped out of the car, the smell of the salt air being bought in by the easterly breeze was comforting somehow.

Morgan slipped into his dress blues jacket and stepped around the back of the car, as I put on my sport coat. It had been more years than I realized since I'd seen Morgan in his dress uniform. The left side of his jacket held an incredible display of ribbons, medals, and accommodations. He discussed any details of his time in the service so little, I felt a pang of guilt that I had forgotten just how decorated a soldier my twin brother was. Morgan kept himself in such great shape, the twenty-year-old uniform fit him like it had been tailored for him the day before. I stepped up to him and removed a speck of lint off his right upper arm sleeve.

"You're representing your country, the navy, and Sims very well today, brother."

Morgan placed his cover squarely on his head, insuring it was precisely positioned. Then together, we walked side by side to the gravesite, surrounded by four servicemen in matching dress blues and a navy chaplain.

The chaplain spoke all the appropriate words without the need of notes, as he'd no doubt given this speech many more times than he would ever have wished to. A prayer was given, followed by a short beat of silence. The bugler slowly raised his horn and with crystal like clarity, the sound of taps reverberated across the hallowed ground, carried along by the cool of the shade and morning air.

The precision the two uniformed sailors demonstrated folding the American flag draped on the coffin was beautiful in a strange way. So careful, so reverent. These men didn't know Sims. Never met him, even. The only thing they needed to know was that he served. After a crisp military turn, the flag was handed to the fourth sailor that formally spun and approached Morgan. He turned precisely to face Morgan and extended his hands, holding the flag.

"In honor of the service to a grateful nation."

Morgan took the flag, and the sailor snapped to attention, saluting. Morgan shifted the flag to his left hand and returned the salute.

Morgan and I quietly shook hands and thanked the members of the honor guard and walked slowly back to the car. We both hung our jackets in the back seat and got in. I started the engine and slipped the car into drive, ready to head south and get out of these clothes.

"I need to make one more stop, this morning," Morgan said.

"Where to?" I asked.

"Miami airport."

I put the car back in park and turned to my brother. "Where you headed?"

"Vega is not going to stop, Michael."

"Okay then, let's go."

Morgan shook his head. "No. The crew needs you, and someone has to start looking for our next project. I love the life we're building and we need expeditions to fund it."

"Bullshit! I'm not letting you go alone."

"Look, I am very proud of you and the skills you've developed. You're not just a boat captain and an amazing cinematographer anymore, you're becoming a hands down, emerging badass. But you're just not quite ready . . . for this."

I was furious and insulted, or maybe more truthfully, I was hurt. Add to that, I was scared of all the ramifications this conversation may have.

"Where and how—"

Morgan answered my unfinished questions. "I made some calls and two former operators will meet me in Miami, and we'll take a private hop into a base in central Mexico. CISEN will provide some equipment and pick up the expenses. Look, when I left the DEV Group, I never thought I'd be part of something that I was as proud of as the work we did there. But you've changed all that. I'm proud of what we're doing. For the first time in a while, I'm really excited about the future. Your leadership and skills are going to take us far. That's what you're good at. And I'm good at protecting what we've built. So that's what I'm going to do. I'll be back before the New Year."

"And if you're not?"

Morgan didn't miss a beat. "You'll be the eldest brother of our family. And the captain of a capable crew and worthy vessel. You'll do what a Gannon shouldered with those responsibilities does."

The statement took me aback at first. But then it seeped in as truthful as knowing your own name. It was exactly what I'd do and I knew it, even though I still wanted to fight it. I wanted to hash out a dozen other possible scenarios. I wanted any solution other than this one. But like so many situations throughout our lives as brothers, Morgan had carefully weighed the options and thought this through step-by-step. And as much as it always galled me, in my gut, I knew he was right.

"You've dropped me at the airport like this a dozen times, Michael. I was deployed a lot over the years. This is no different."

I gave him the look, and Morgan looked away, straight out through the windshield.

"Okay, yeah . . . this is different. But it's no less necessary."

We both sat quietly watching the morning sun filter through the shade canopy of the giant Banyans, dappling the markers across the memorial garden with shimmering flecks of gold and white. It was a beautiful scene, but I couldn't help but think that this was the worst place in the world to have this conversation. Wanting to normalize the moment anyway I could, I finally broke the silence with a mundane question. "You need any gear from the boat?"

"My go bag is in the trunk. I couldn't sleep, so I loaded it last night."

Totally surprised that I missed any sign of him loading anything, I asked, "So when did you decide to go?"

"When I closed the door on the ambulance that took Mateo away."

I recalled the chaos of the scene. The victims being treated on the ground, and Mateo's burned face. Then the words he whispered with complete confidence: "We'll get her." I silently nodded and put the car into drive, headed for the airport.

Chapter 22

TWO DAYS BEFORE CHRISTMAS, I sat on the boarding steps of *Water Horse*, nursing my first cup of coffee with a full thermos beside me. We docked in a marina that catered to more work boats than tourists, so the predawn activity on the dock was brisk, with men and women starting their day fishing, crabbing, and lobstering. I enjoyed watching the early marina bustle. Most mornings, I'd meet a new waterman when I'd offer to top off his insulated mug that seemed permanently affixed to most hands out on the dock at this time of morning. This morning was no different. A young man trying to wipe the previous night out of his eyes, yawned his way down the dock.

"Morning, Captain," he said.

"How'd you know I was the captain?" I asked.

"Got the look." He smiled.

"Want a top off on that mug, sailor?"

"That'd be great," he said as he came up and parked on the step next to me.

I poured him a refill and he replaced the lid on his travel mug. "Thank you, Captain."

"Michael Gannon," I said, extending my hand.

"Nice to meet you, Michael. Nate Whitman."

"Where's home, Nate?"

"Washington state, mostly. I'm on the run from the gloom for a few months. Down here just working as a mate on a charter boat down the dock."

He looked at the Water Horse logo on my shirt and said, "Hey, you ever worked with the guys from Sea Watcher?"

I laughed. "As a matter of fact, I have. How do you know those boys?"

"I just finished a job with them. Sammy Daniels and I have become great buddies. Wow, what a small world."

Life on the water was a small world. Even with as many boats, mariners, and ports there were in the world, it wasn't uncommon to run into old acquaintances, no matter where you found yourself, if you were standing on a dock.

"How are the boys doing?" I asked.

"Doing great. Headed for a job in Hawaii. They made me

an offer, but I'm trying to learn the charter business. I'm saving every dime I can to start a charter business next fall. Sammy says he'll come mate for me."

"Just keep him fed and you'll be fine," I said, smiling.

"Well, thanks for the refill, Michael. Great to meet you. Wow, that is so weird, you know Sammy."

"Nah, just a waterway thing, Nate. Very nice to meet you. Be safe out there and keep your head down and get that business started next fall."

"I will, thanks, Captain." And he was off down the dock for a long day on the water.

Christmas in the Keys was, well . . . different. Christmas trees were strings of lighted fishing buoys strung lengthwise off tall pilings in the shape of a tree. Or my favorite, lighted lobster traps stacked in a circular birthday cake fashion, to make the shape of the Yuletide icon. Santa looked different as well. There was plenty of long white hair and beards around town, but the heavy red fleece proved too hot for the climate. Instead, Santa donned topical shirts, board shorts, flip-flops. And one that I'll never be able to unsee—a speedo wearing Santa with suspenders and full-color Rudolf painted on his chest and large belly.

One highlight was the lighted boat parade. If it floated and you could string lights on it, it was in the floating "boat" parade. With the new low-power LED lights, the possibilities for lighting schemes were endless. It was a treat to witness and was as much a part of the soul of the Keys as Hemingway and conch shells.

Ellie stepped down one step and joined me. She didn't say anything, she just extended her empty mug in my direction and I silently poured her cup full. I let her get one large sip before I spoke. "Morning, sis. Late night?"

"I'm almost finished. I need to recheck a few sources and tighten up the last paragraph, and I'll submit it. It's a shame there was so much evidence destroyed, I'd really like to have nailed Vega. But there's enough here to send Goddard scrambling for a while."

"That's good," I said.

"Heard anything from Morgan?"

"Not yet. He took the Sims thing pretty hard. He just needed a few days alone to process it. A few days of fishing and quietly re-striping and re-cleaning a handgun or two for the tenth time will put him back on track. He'll be here before the New Year." I desperately hoped.

"You're probably right. I worry about him though," she said.

"Scoot over, you two."

I looked up and Rudy stood above us, his arm in a sling and an empty cup in his good right hand. Ellie and I slid further apart and Rudy came down a step and sat, repeating the silent mug extend. I poured him full and he took a sip.

"Not bad," he said. I rolled my eyes and El snickered.

"You know, we have chairs on the deck," Rudy murmured.

"I like the steps, when we're in port. It's quiet," I said, turning to face him.

"Mmm," he said, taking another sip. "Not bad at all."

The morning sun had chased away the predawn and the low golden rays sparkled across the clear water of the basin. I looked down the long dock leading from the parking lot and caught a sight that never failed to make me smile. Mom and Dad coming down the dock. Mom carried her purse, while Dad pulled a dock cart stacked chest high with suit-cases and brown grocery bags. The three of us stood and stepped down onto the dock. Ellie closed the distance and met them both with hugs. As I stepped up, Mom patted me on the face.

"Hey, son, Christmas together was a great idea. Your dad has been packed for a week."

"I'm really glad you're here, Mom."

She cocked her head as she met my eyes. "You okay? Where's your brother?"

"He needed a few days after we buried his friend. He'll be here soon."

She held eye contact a little longer, putting the mother super-BS meter to work and decided to give me a temporary pass. "Help your dad with the stuff, will you?"

"Momma Gannon," Rudy exclaimed.

"Rudy, how are you healing, dear?" she asked.

"Doin' just fine, but I'm glad you're here." He leaned a little closer and mock whispered, "Your kids are going to starve us to death."

"Hey!" I said.

"I'm kidding. The casseroles were good—the first three times."

"Don't you worry, Rudy. I stopped at the grocery and got plenty."

Dad confirmed the morning chores as he shook his head in resignation. "Yep, we brought most of the store with us," he said.

Mom and Rudy scuttled off. He was Mom's favorite, and she enjoyed pampering "her stand-in" when she wasn't around.

I stepped up to Dad and hugged him. "Hey Pop. Glad you're here too. Just leave the cart, I'll get the guys to help me unload it."

"Morgan really okay?" he asked with his voice lowered.

"He'll be fine, Dad. He'll be back in a few days."

Satisfied, he stepped around me and put his arm around Ellie as they climbed the boarding steps. "Tell me how the article is coming," he asked, as they walked up the side deck.

It had been a week since I'd had any communication with Morgan. I got a text from him just before he and his team departed the covert base in central Mexico, saying they had a few leads. But since then, nothing. The boat wasn't the same without him. A balance was missing and I think we could all feel it. More than that, he was my brother and our connection was strong. I wouldn't be able to rest until I saw him coming down the dock, unshaven with his seabag on his shoulder.

Beau stepped out on deck and stretched. "Morning, Cap, need some help there?"

"Yeah, that'd be great. I think Mom bought half of Tom Thumb Foods."

"I could already hear the pots rattling in the galley on my way out." He laughed.

Over the next two days, I made a few calls to inquire about potential work for the new year, and Mom and one-armed Rudy kept us overfed and relaxed. We enjoyed the mild sunny days and afternoon walks along the docks. Dad and I loved to walk the docks together, and as we walked and talked about all the different boats, he caught me up on all the scuttlebutt from the Low Country. He was excited about the new fishing skiff he was building out back. Twenty-one foot, with twin four-stroke one-fifties. We made plans for Morgan and me to come home and help him launch it late spring. As we walked along, he sensed my heaviness. "You worried about him?"

I didn't answer right away. Then I said, "A little."

"I think your brother came out of the womb taking care of himself. He'll be okay, son."

"I know, Pop. I'd be better if we were all together for Christmas."

"Not the first time, kid. But we'll just keep stealing times together whenever we can."

Christmas afternoon, I declared the galley closed and I rounded up our gang and we invaded a local spot that specialized in hogfish. You didn't normally catch a hogfish on a hook and line, they were always speared. They had a strange set of upturned lips and face, thus the name. The rustic eatery and bar could prepare the white-fleshed fish in almost endless ways and all of them were delicious. We ate and drank ice cold beer, and Mom got a kick out of sharing pictures on her phone of Morgan and me as kids with Jas. The two pointed and laughed, and I was sure I'd never live some of it down.

We ambled back to the boat, trying to walk off some of the meal, as dusk settled over the island. Jas had gone into town a few days before and bought a dozen boxes of Christmas lights in an "everything must go" sale. When we rounded the corner, the results of her labor lit up the end of the dock. *Water Horse* resting in her berth now glowed, bedazzled from stem to stern with blinking red and green lights.

"It's beautiful, Jas," Mom said.

"Merry Christmas, everybody," Jas said.

"Merry Christmas!" we all replied.

The group stood and took in the scene. Then one by one, ambled up the boarding steps and into the boat. I stayed behind and sat on the steps. The stars were beginning to twinkle into view as the sky became fully dark. You could hear Christmas music coming from a few boats in the marina, along with laughing and quiet conversations, as the cooler night air carried subtle sounds across the still basin. My cell phone buzzed, startling me, and I scrambled to pull it from my pocket. It was a text message from Morgan. I was almost afraid to read it. I touched the alert and the message appeared on the screen.

Getting closer. Sorry I'm missing the celebration. Tell Mom and Dad I'm fine. Got a call from a buddy at Naval Command about previously undiscovered German U-boats off the coast of Louisiana. Video call with them in a few weeks.

I read the message twice. I was grateful to hear from him, but it wasn't the Christmas present I was hoping for.

I typed back: *Better hurry, pie going fast. One of Mom's best. Merry Christmas, brother.*

There was no reply.

"You okay?" Jas asked, as she sat down on the step beside me.

"Not the message I'd hoped for, but something, at least." I handed her my phone with the message still on the screen. She read and smiled, then handed me back the phone. We both sat there in the quiet for a moment.

"I'm not sure what I'll do if he doesn't come back," I finally said.

Jas reached and put her hand on top of mine. "He's coming back, Michael. But if God forbid, he didn't, you know what we'd do. We'd cry and mourn, then celebrate him by recognizing that he made each of us a little stronger because he was a part of us. Then, we'd keep doing what we were made to do. Morgan is giving this family the best gift he knows how to give."

I felt a single tear spill from my right eye and I wiped it away. Jas turned to me and touched my chin, turning my face toward her. She leaned in and kissed me gently on the lips, then looked into my eyes. "Merry Christmas, Michael." Then she stood to walk back inside.

"Merry Christmas, Jas."

Alone again on the steps, I looked up into the night sky, trying to picture where Morgan was and what he was doing at that moment. "I'll see you soon, brother," I said aloud. My phone pinged in my hand and I looked at the screen:

Merry Christmas, Michael.

Author's Note

Bermeja is, or was, a real island according to the Mexican government and it was identified on numerous charts from antiquity and again verified on a survey in the twentieth century. In the 1990s when territorial waters were being evaluated to determine oil exploration rights, the island could not be found. This is still a mystery. I pushed the later survey dates into the 2000s to make the story work. It's also true that there have even been a few outlandish conspiracy theories tossed about concerning the disappearance of the tiny island. And although I have no doubt that there have been schemes and plans that border on the edge of legality around the world of petroleum and energy exploration and mining, everything in this story has been fabricated from my imagination.

It's also true that there are many limestone caverns under the seafloor of the Gulf of Mexico. Particularly around the Yucatán Peninsula. However, it's unlikely, but not impossible, that any of them would contain the right conditions for lithium to be present. I just like the idea of the double cross, so when my research indicated "possible," I indulged.

If you are ever about to step into a watering hole on your travels, remember the rule: Windows, good. No windows, bad. There is a local restaurant on Stock Island that has the most incredible hogfish . . . anything in the world. Ask anyone on the island and they'll get you there.

I hope you'll continue to follow Michael and the whole crew of Water Horse Expeditions on future waterway adventures. Look for my next book in the series, under the working title of *Old Gray Wolves*, coming soon.

If you'd like a free book, come visit my website at matthewgorebooks.com and download the free e-book or audiobook entitled *Clear Waters*. It's a short novella origin story of Michael's career as a conflict journalist and his journey to find new adventure and a new home, aboard *Water Horse*.

About the Author

MATTHEW GORE is a 30-year-veteran video director and editor and sought after storyteller whose talents transcend both the screen and the page. His work has earned him multiple prestigious awards in the world of television and video production

Self-proclaimed as nautically obsessed, Matthew and his enterprising wife, Darla, moved aboard their beautiful fantail trawler, *Ancient Mariner*, to experience a life tempo unique only to living on the water.

Matthew's love for the sea and adventure shines through in his ocean-based action-adventure "Waterway Chronicle" books. In these gripping tales, readers follow the exploits of Michael and Morgan Gannon, aboard their home, the one-hundred-forty-foot ship *Water Horse*, that serves as the base for Water Horse Expeditions.

With each page, Matthew takes you along with his cast of characters into a world of thrilling escapades and nautical mysteries that unfold against a backdrop of waves, gadgets, and guns on the boundless oceans and waterways of the world. Dive into the excitement and shove off with Matthew on the next Waterway Chronicle Adventure.

Made in the USA
Middletown, DE
20 December 2024

67855107R00146